THE WORD CATCHER

A NOVEL

BY
Patricia A. Florio

THE WORD CATCHER

Copyright © 2024 Patricia A. Florio

Publisher Information

America Publishers
Email: info@americapublishers.com
Phone: +1 (617) 334-5774

ISBN Information

eBook: 978-1-966198-09-3
Paperback: 978-1-966198-07-9
Hardcover: 978-1-966198-08-6

Cover Design by: America Publishers

Printed in the United States of America

1st Edition: November, 2024

TABLE OF CONTENTS

Part I Foundations of Faith..1

Prologue 2

Chapter 1 5

Chapter 2.. 12

Chapter 3 28

Chapter 4 33

Chapter 5 38

Chapter 6 42

Chapter 7... 53

Chapter 8 55

Chapter 9 62

Chapter 10... 68

Chapter 11... 77

Chapter 12 88

Part II Family Secrets **93**

Chapter 1 94

Chapter 2.. 100

Chapter 3 104

Chapter 4 109

Chapter 5 114

Chapter 6 117

Chapter 7..124

Part III Temptation Happens To The Best Humans **126**

Chapter 1... 127

Chapter 2..136

Chapter 3 141

Part IV Costa And Agnes Reunite....................................**153**

Chapter 1 154

Part V Good Advice **160**

Chapter 1...161

Chapter 2..166

Chapter 3 173

About the Author 175

PART I

FOUNDATIONS OF FAITH

PROLOGUE

Early on a Sunday morning in September 1965, Costa and Maria Lewis, pushed their infant daughter in a royal blue pram to the Cathedral on the Hill, an affluent Catholic church located in the Garden District of New Orleans.

Maria Lewis and the baby's godmother, Genevieve Rosa, had earlier that morning, dressed the baby in a satin christening gown, which they embellished with strands of pink ribbon that flowed beneath the infant's dimpled knees.

Inside the church, the altar was decorated with vases of white flowers to signify the purity of an innocent child. Standing to the right of the baptismal font, Maria softly rocked the child in her arms. A kaleidoscope of colors filtered through the stained-glass windows.

Among the first sentences the priest uttered sounded rather austere to the parents and godparents. He posed this question to them on behalf of the newly inducted child.

"Do you renounce Satan and all of his empty promises?"

The parents and godparents answered in unison, "Yes, we do renounce Satan and all of his empty promises." He pointed to the godparents, and Maria handed the baby to Genevieve.

"Will you raise this child in the Roman Catholic faith should, God forbid, something has happened to her parents?'

"Yes, we will," the godparents answered.

As life-long members of the Catholic church, the parents and godparents, had witnessed other baptisms and understood the ritual of the sacrament; that the newly christened child's soul was now wiped clean of the stain of Original Sin.

Catholics have always believed that this curse of original sin had been gifted by the first parents, Adam and Eve, because they were tempted by Satan in the Garden of Eden to eat the Fruit of Knowledge.

The austere pastor, Father Jacque, poured holy water on top of the child's head and anointed her forehead with the oils of salvation, tracing with his thumb the sign of the cross.

A flash bulb temporarily blinded those standing at the altar when a photographer snapped a picture of baby's head while being doused with holy water. Maria dried the baby's delicate scalp and placed a satin bonnet over the baby's fine ginger hair.

On the steps outside of church, several more pictures were taken. Arturo Rosa smiled into the camera, a toothy grin, proud of his role as the godfather to his very first granddaughter.

As the attendees of the baptism walked down the long set of concrete steps of the Cathedral, Arturo sidled up to Costa, handing him a sizeable check made payable in the baby's name.

Costa kissed Arturo on both cheeks, placed the check inside his pocket next to a note that he had received earlier that morning from Agnes, Maria's cousin, who was intentionally not invited to attend the christening.

Arturo ushered his family with a wave of his hands, *Andiamo!*" he said, "Everyone to the bakery for a celebration."

And in this way Maria-Elaina, who would be known throughout her life as Lana, was ushered into the family.

Chapter 1

**Almost Forty Years Later
June 16, 1999**

*The devil is not in the details, but in the
temptations that he offers.*

Maria Rosa-Lewis

Lana raced down the marble steps, grabbing on tightly to the banister, hoping to prevent from falling. She hurried through the main lobby of Brooklyn's Kings County Municipal building, exiting the front door, falling between the crowds on the sidewalk, as if she were exiting a burning building.

She continued her sprint heading across Court Street, traversing Montague Street. Her destination Chase Bank.

She had little time. She was scheduled to work at nine o'clock sharp inside the grand jury located on the first floor of Supreme Court and it already?? (time). The damning envelope that she had discovered that morning in her correspondence box was stuffed inside her clothing. She could almost feel it????? Surely Jay Larkin, the vice president of Chase Bank, and an old friend would know what to do. As she sprinted across the street, she sent up a prayer for Larkin's, and God's, guidance.

A foul stench emanated from the sewer as Lana stepped off the curb, pushing towards oncoming traffic. The humidity and stink weakened Lana's stomach. She shoved her hands over her mouth and pushed on faster.

A heat advisory had been posted that morning cautioning the elderly and infirmed to remain indoors and to drink plenty of water.

Lana had ignored these warnings. She was under forty-years-old and didn't believe the cautions pertained to her. Yet, her heart beat wildly in her chest. But southbound cars moved at a rapid pace, jumping in between.

An annoyed uniformed police officer waved her through.

With only forty-five minutes between her and the time to start her job as a court reporter, she raced inside the doors of the bank. A strange man held his arms out like a tool taker, preventing her from entering the bank.

"Hey, lady, watch where you're going," he said. The frustrated old geezer said Lana had bumped into him. She muttered an apology, which he refused to accept. She hadn't *meant* to cause him to lose his footing. He persisted in not letting her into the door of the bank.

Lana rolled her eyes at him; he threw up his hands and let her to get inside the door, still making a fuss. The extra minutes wasted added to the drama in an already dramatic situation.

Once inside, the air conditioning felt calming on her sweat-drenched body. She paced herself now, with a steady clip-clop, clip-clop, her heels tapping out the slower beat on the white marble floor.

Lana approached Teller Number 1, standing behind the window sipping something cold from a straw.

"Can you tell me if Jay Larkin is in?" she asked, almost apologetic, because he had to remove the straw from his mouth to answer her question. He pointed Lana towards the back of the bank where a row of offices was situated. She thanked him and walked in the direction as the vaulted ceiling picked up the music of her beige high heels.

Seated behind a sleek mahogany desk, Jay Larkin, a sixty-year-old banking veteran, was reading *The New York Times*. He raised his eyes when he saw Lana approaching.

"Well, how are you luv?" he said, smiling and pushing aside the newspaper.

Lana didn't answer but silently removing the black tote bag from her shoulder. She reach inside, pulled out a white envelope, and tossed it in his direction. The envelope slid open revealing a thick stack of one-hundred-dollar bills.

"Well, top of the mornin' to you too, luv." Larkin said with a lilt of the old country in his tone.

"Take a look at this bullshit," she said. Jay stared at her, not understanding what she meant.

"What bullshit is that, dear?" he humored her. "This envelope that you've *rudely* tossed at me?"

Lana's face flushed. She nodded at him, now feeling ashamed of her actions, her neck turning pink and hot.

Larkin still didn't understand what was going on as he eyed the Ben Franklins.

"For fuck's sake, luv, out with it," he said. "What's this is all about?"

Lana's legs gave way and she slid into the brown leather chair on the opposite side of the desk.

"A fuckin bribe," she said. "Someone left me a fuckin bribe!" Larkin looked confused. Mouth agape, he stammered.

"Wha--what are you talking about, what kind of bribe?"

Lana pointed to the note sticking out of the envelope. "Read that," she said.

Jay removed the slip of paper. He read the words that were neatly printed aloud. "*Ms. Lewis, destroy your notes from June 6, 1999 on the indictment of Niccolo Giovanni. Please provide action to this simple request.*"

"Clean, precise and to the point," he said. Their eyes locked onto one another's. Her greenish eyes looked like the color of a frozen lime Popsicle.

Larkin muttered, "According to this note—as it reads – you are being offered this money, *when* you lose your grand jury notes, not *if* you lose them."

They searched one another's faces. His watery blue eyes focused on hers. She could see he understood the meaning of a bribe. He had also registered that it was against the law to bribe someone. The written instructions hadn't said why she should lose the indictment notes, just that she ought to.

As a seven-year veteran, working for the District Attorney's office, Lana had never been bribed. Ever. Her stomach was doing flips, just like when it's said to have butterflies in your stomach.

Lana said, "I don't know a Niccolo Giovanni. I can't even imagine why he picked me. All I can think of is mafia. You know what I'm saying? An Italian name like Giovanni, that's my first guess. That he's Mafia. I can't remember being the grand jury reporter on any Mafia cases recently. That's something I'd remember."

Larkin didn't say a word. But she said, she'd know for sure. While it all sounded reasonable, he didn't know what to think.

Lana continued. "You know, I've been helping Vince in his courtroom one day a week. I've been spending less time working in the grand jury. I mean, I know for sure I was there on June 6, because Vince hadn't started treatment until after that date."

Larkin listened as the words flowed out of Lana's mouth. Ever so gently while she spoke, he pushed the envelope back in her direction. His watery blue eyes seemed faraway like in *Never Never Land*, because he hadn't a clue as to what her job entailed; he wasn't a hundred percent sure that he understood what an indictment was. He knew she was a court stenographer on murder cases, and things like that, using that little machine that looked like a truncated typewriter. But that was all he knew about her job.

"It doesn't make sense," she said. "When I got to my office this morning, I searched inside my correspondence box for my keys. They weren't there. I dumped the whole box on my desk and that's when this white envelope fell out."

"What are you going to do?" Larkin asked. "I mean, there's got to be somebody you could go to in the DA's office, you know, speak to a detective. Let them know about what you've found this morning. I'm sure bribing a court reporter must be against the law."

Of course, it was against the law. She knew the penal code backwards and forward. She had probably taken dictation on charges related to bribes. She had known beforehand that it was a felony to bribe someone. Especially under these circumstance, asking an official of the court to lose grand jury notes.

"I can't figure out how someone got into my cubicle. I mean, cubicles aren't ever locked. But how someone got into my office, the DA's office no less, stole my keys that lock and unlock my drawer, left an envelope full of one-hundred-dollar bills without anyone seeing them? The whole thing is bizarre."

Larkin puckered up his lips. *Bizarre, good word, he thought. Exactly. And as a good friend of her husband's, was she thinking I can do something about this?*

CHAPTER 2

Jay Larkin recalled the first time he had met Lana; it was the day her husband Vince had taken her to Chase bank to add her as a signatory on his business accounts. Vince had become friends with Larkin. They had ridden the train together to and from work, getting off, or on, at the Clark Street station in downtown Brooklyn.

One morning, it caught Larkin's attention that Vince had lose a lot of weight. He didn't want to ask the guy what was going on. It was that afternoon Vince had brought his wife to the bank.

Larkin remembered standing up, welcoming the couple into his office and how the striking, petite ginger-headed woman had made an impression on him. Vince had made the introductions.

"Jay, this is my wife Lana. Lana, meet Mr. Larkin, a really great guy," Vince said smiling a generous smile.

The business-dressed female looked more like a teenage girl than a fully-grown woman and mother of eighteen-year-old twins.

Lana reached out her hand, taking Larkin's in hers.

She had soft hands, warm to the touch. The palest green eyes. Her suit was the color of orange sorbet. They were seated; Larkin behind his desk, the couple in front, while Larkin selected the index cards, the customary signatory ones, which he had retrieved prior for Mrs. Scotto to fill out and sign.

Clicking open a ball-point pen, Lana filled in the blanks. Larkin noticed Lana had printed her first name as Marie-Elaina. On the second line, she wrote Lewis-Scotto. Larkin made a mental note: the first time he had never seen anyone fill the spaces with two hyphenated names.

What he had taken from this first meeting was that he liked Lana. The fact that she had reached out to shake his hand made an impression on him. He hadn't had many women shake his hand. Larkin thought Lana was one of those woman's libbers, outgoing, confident, different from his own wife, who liked being old fashioned.

Although, she looked like a grown-up Barbie Doll, she didn't interrupt her husband when he was speaking, explaining why the changes on the signatory cards.

"I'm going to be away almost every Thursday through Monday for six months," Vince said.

Lana remained silent, watching her husband, with what Larkin thought were tears welling up in her eyes.

"I want Lana to be able to sign paychecks for my employees."

Larkin hadn't been aware, Vince would be starting chemotherapy for a form of lung cancer.

Larkin presented a longer sheet of paper for Vince and Lana to sign, giving Lana the authority to sign paychecks in Vince's absence.

As instructed by Larkin, she printed her full name, hyphenated, first and last names, then signed in all four places.

"You know they are used to receiving their checks on Fridays and hard-pressed if they don't."

Larkin smiled. Weekly Friday paychecks were rare in any business. Most companies were on a bi-monthly basis.

"I don't see any problem," he said.

Then asked Vince a strange question. "Will you be working in Philadelphia for a few weeks?"

Remembering Vince had travelled for another court reporter agency on Market Street, a high-powered agency, when the girls planned on living on campus in Binghamton, New York.

Lana looked across at her husband. She realized Vince hadn't told Larkin about his present illness.

"Yes," Vince said. "I'll be away on Fridays for a few months," he said, while pushing back a strand of dark hair that had fallen over his right eye.

Lana noticed Vince looking awkward and lying about his present situation. She then decided to take up the conversation.

"Mr. Larkin," she said in a clear and stable tone, "my husband will be starting treatment for lung cancer. I'm going to be filling in his courtroom once and a while and will take care of the banking."

Lana patted Vince's right hand and then held it tight.

"We wanted some privacy," she said to Larkin.

She didn't know why she said that. And she didn't know why she was taking a picture out of her wallet of their twin daughters to show to Larkin.

Lana had made the decision on the spur of the moment after having observed Larkin in the father role from the pictures with his wife and six children hanging on the wall behind his desk. It was easy to tell from the picture, who they had taken after, blonde, blue-eyed, a variety of children, toddlers to teenagers.

Larkin instinctively poured Vince a glass of water from a silver pitcher on his desk. He felt terrible for the young man who was sitting before him; who couldn't possibly have been older more than forty-five years old.

Vince sipped the water and thanked Larkin. Lana put the picture back in her wallet and finished signing the forms allowing her authorization to sign checks on behalf of Vince's agency, Five Borough Court Reporting Services.

Lana, in a polite conversation that ensured afterwards, arranged to stop in and see Larkin, promising she'd keep him updated on her husband.

Lana held on to Vince as he struggled rise from the chair. They all stared at one another intently, almost like waiting for another secret to be told. But that secret was already out of the bag. Larkin was the first person outside of Vince's office with whom Lana had confided in about her husband's illness. The court reporters' world was a small one. Once news got out about Vince's illness, Lana would be plagued by phone calls and well-wishers. Nothing in the world of court reporting ever stayed a secret.

On the walk back to Vince's office on Clinton Street, Lana thought about some of the old sayings her mother used to repeat: "Life's a bitch and then you die." There were loads of others in Maria's lexicon of irony: "You never know what's going to happen to you from one moment to the next." The best one she heard her mother repeat often, Lana hadn't understood when she was a child, and she wasn't sure she understood it now: "The devil is not in the details. The devil is in the temptations."

$$*****$$

Now, two weeks later, sitting across from Jay as he nervously tapped the bulging envelope, Lana began to consider some of her mother's old sayings......That last one about the devil not being in the details was the saying that most affected Lana at present. One moment, she's sharing her husband's cancer with Larkin. Several weeks later, she's sitting at his desk shaking in her shoes, begging him: *Help me, do something, relieve me of whatever this is. I can't do it alone.*"

She also realized, Larkin wasn't eager to take this on.

He had kept his hands folded in front of him at the desk, trying terribly hard not to scratch the itch needling him from a rash that always seemed to be present at the thought of doing the wrong thing.

He wanted to tell Lana to call her husband. But he knew that wasn't even an option. The man had his own problems. He knew she had no one else to go to. *But why him?*

After her initial meeting with Jay, she seemed to run into him all the time. Lana had been crossing over Court Street, from the DA's office, to become bookkeeper in her husband's office and had run into him. Several mornings on the Clark Street station together they'd also run in to one another and laugh. It had become a habit – or was it that Lana took the same train as Larkin?

To be a nice guy, One day, Larkin had invited Lana to have a coffee with him sitting on the stools at the counter of the Greek diner on Cadman Plaza.

Lana had never spoken of her grand jury cases with Larkin. But they did share novels that they had both read in the past. The one Lana couldn't stop talking about was *Crime and Punishment*. Larkin thought Dostoyevsky was a bit over his head. Didn't she get enough crime on her job?

"I thought I had heard everything about crime and punishment there was to tell," she had said, "you know, me working in the grand jury, but this book has boggled my mind."

"How so?" Larkin asked, intrigued by her word boggled.

"It's epic, dealing with a man who had made a decision to steal back his father's watch that he had pawned with his landlady – Russia, Nineteenth Century – but he's angry by the jewels she had taken from people and had given them very little in the way of compensation. Being so enraged by her selfishness, he kills her and kills her servant girl. I mean, he brutally kills them. He seemed like such a nice man at the beginning of the story, not anyone who would commit a crime of that magnitude."

"Heat of the moment?" Larkin asked.

"I guess," she said. "The landlady was a pawn broker and he judged her unfairness to regular people, starving people, without enough money to eat or afford shelter."

"Does he get caught?"

"Hmm, eventually," she said "But it goes on and on, so many chapters, so many characters; his mother, his sister, women, men of that era. Dostoyevsky, I think, was a genius."

She had then started to share some interesting scenes from her own cases, never naming names from her early days as a stenographer in the homicide division."

"You've actually witnessed dead bodies?" Larkin asked.

"Murdered bodies," she corrected, adding, "Many times." She said this nonchalantly like they were taking about a movie and not real live murders.

That's when Larkin realized Lana had taken the blood and gore home with her every night, going back over her day's notes, typing up transcripts of the cases she had reported earlier that morning, watching the scenes play out in her mind again.

"You know," she said. "I never wanted to get involved in this career. Vince talked me into it."

******

Larkin sighed. What were they doing staring at an envelope sitting on his desk like it might jump up and bite one of them on the nose?

Moving back and forth in his chair, he couldn't help thinking: *this money should be easy enough to stash away.*

He brought his seat back up straight and relaxed back into the soft leather of the brown chair. *The crap she must hear every day – certainly not fairytales about unicorns.*

"Why don't you go to your friend the cop, Peter Salazar?" he asked. "He'd certainly know if this Giovanni person was mafia."

Lana looked like she wanted to vomit when Jay uttered Salazar's name. Larkin accepted her cold stare, but wondered, *What? Did I say something wrong? Oh, she looks pissed at me.* He was sorry he had opened his mouth.

Lana felt a scream swelling up inside her belly that felt on fire. Salazar had been a sore subject in the Scotto household almost from the second month she had worked as a homicide steno.

What if she jumped up and down like a spoiled brat, could she then force Larkin to listen, do something with the money she had thrown on his desk? But she knew she could never do that. She felt suffocated, stamped out like a burning fire, almost as if she had no emotions at all. Her hands felt ice cold. She felt numb. Though she pondered Larkin's suggestion to go to Salazar.

"If I go to the police, they're going to want to question me, take me out of the grand jury – I can't do that right now – I need to work. I only get paid a salary when I work. They're going to want me to fill out a report, answer a million questions."

She was about to cry and sucked down hard, composing herself. "I don't have any answers for them. I only have questions, too." Larkin nodded his head, supporting her theory.

"This guy, the one in the note, Niccolo Giovanni. Do you know him?"

"Of course, I don't know him. I could only guess I had been the reporter at his indictment. Why else would someone send a stack of money to me on his behalf? It doesn't make sense."

She glanced behind Larkin and saw the small silver safe that had always been situated there. It made her mind start calculating.

"I believe you, Lana," Larkin said, signaling with his hand, for her to keep her voice down. She couldn't help focusing on the safe behind him.

She said, "Did I tell you my keys were missing?"

"What keys?" he asked.

"The keys I keep hidden inside my correspondence box. They open the drawer where my grand jury notes are stored. This morning, instead of keys I found the envelope."

He looked confused, not totally understanding what she was talking about. What else hadn't she told him? All this cloak and dagger, keys, bribes, grand juries, mafia. It made him feel jumpy: Were cops going to bust into the bank and arrest them both?

Lana wiggled in her seat. She felt Larkin's eyes on her, searching her every move. Tension mounted inside the small office surrounded with files and boxes, and a small safe located behind the man with whom she was now pleading her case.

That comment she had made: The reporter who had taken the Giovanni indictment. He thought that made sense. *Why else would someone drop off all this money to a court reporter and place it inside her correspondence box?*

"No clue. I swear," Lana said. "My routine is the same every day when I go into the office. I stick my fingers in the correspondence box, fish around for my keys, pull them out and open my desk drawer. Today, I found this."

She then repeated it again to hear her own voice sound out something unrealistic as finding an envelope filled with hundred-dollar bills. It was just like a scene from *Law and Order*. Certainly not the way her day generally started.

"Jay, this is out of left-field," she said. "I'm in serious shit."

For the first time, Larkin thought he had spotted tears begin to well up in her eyes. It must have been the realization of the magnitude of receiving a bribe.

"Please," she stammered, "I...I need your help."

"I wish I could help you, luv, but I can't," Larkin whispered, afraid their conversation was getting too loud again. He pushed the white envelope back in her direction. "Take this over one of detectives."

She looked at him, not with contempt, but with the realization that he was right. She hated her stubborn determination when she got her Irish up; when she wanted a situation to go her way. The loud voice in her head said: *You better not give this money to a detective, not until you've had an opportunity to talk it over with Vince.*

"I can't do anything about this today," she announced, convinced of her own words. "I should wait until Monday when my Rob, my supervisor, comes back from vacation. Just help me for a few days. I can't trust anyone else." Her voice trembled.

Larkin heard something in her tone he hadn't heard until now: Fear. Tears spilled down both her cheeks.

Larkin began to wiggle in his chair. He felt the rash rising under the back of his collar. He pulled at the knot of his tie, loosened it like a man at the end of his rope.

Lana's emotions pushed harder, the tears flowed. *I'm not paid enough money to have this happen to me.*

Instead of saying those words, she picked up the envelope, feeling the thickness and weight of the money inside. She looked down at the white envelope in her hand. She saw Benjamin Franklin's eyes staring back at hers.

"What if I do what I do this? You know, lose my notes? Tell my supervisor I can't find them; somebody took my keys. It is possible, you know, somebody went through that drawer already and found what they were looking for."

Larkin couldn't believe she was saying this. He opened his mouth to speak.

"Wait, wait," she said.

He put up his hand for her to stop talking; they were getting louder again. He moved closer to her, leaning across the desk.

"What happens in case you can't find your notes? Does that mean this Giovanni guy gets to walk, doesn't get indicted because the minutes of the hearing were lost, and the grand jury hearing can't be proven?"

"Not at all," she said. She had known from being a court reporting student, taking a law class, too, that a defendant always has the presumption of innocence until the end of a trial. She felt flummoxed, blabbering like a jabberwocky to an Irish immigrant about U.S. legal strategy. *What the hell do I know. I'm not an attorney, she thought.*

"I'm sure this has happened before. You know? I can't possibly be the first reporter who has misplaced or lost a pack of notes."

Larkin picked up on that immediately. *She's preparing herself internally, he thought.*

"They have to re-indict him with a new panel of jurors. A prosecutor will get to present the case all over again." Larkin looked confused, not understanding what the hell all of it meant.

"What good does it do for this Giovanni guy to bribe you, ask you to lose your notes, or your ability to transcribe his indictment transcript if he gets a do-over?"

Lana stuck up her index finger halting Larkin to explain further.

"Number one," she said, "it gives his defense attorney more time to research and come up with a better defense. That's my guess. I don't really know the exact rules, but it's like a time- element thing."

Larkin squinted, looking confused again. None of it made any sense. He had never been a juror in the U.S, or in Ireland, nor did he have any idea what rules applied. He noticed a glint of mischief in Lana's dazzling wet eyes. She knew something that she wasn't saying.

"I can't – I don't want to take the money home or have it in my purse riding on the subway. I don't feel safe. God forbid I get held up. There has to be five or ten thousand dollars in this envelope." She looked at him as he thought about what she had just said.

He wondered if she had counted the money and perhaps had a bit of larceny in her blood.

"Jay, I swear I haven't really thought this through. I ran out of my office, almost killed myself running down a flight of steps; stepped out into traffic across Court Street like a blind fool. I almost knocked down a guy outside your bank.

She took in a deep breath, calmed herself, then asked Larkin. "Is it possible for me to leave the money here, at the bank?"

"For fuck's sake, Lana. This is an awful lot for me to digest. We can both get into a lot of trouble. You know that, yeah?" She nodded. She understood totally and completely.

"Look, luv, the only thing I can do," the upbeat-Irish lilt was now gone from his voice, "I'll put this envelope in my office safe, okay? Wait a second—did you count it? You said five, ten thousand dollars. Did you count it?"

She shook her head.

Larkin bit down on his lip, causing his face to grimace.

"Are you listening, girl? For fuck's sake, Lana, do you know how much money is in the envelope?"

"I don't want to know."

"Why, because if you knew how much was in there, you'd find reason to keep it?"

"I have plenty of reasons to keep it," she said with a straight face, staring right back into his eyes.

Larkin didn't give Lana a chance to say another word. He didn't want to hear anymore of her plight that didn't concern him fifteen minutes earlier.

"Listen," he said, "we're not getting anywhere by you being evasive." He glanced at his watch, which prompted Lana to look at hers.

"Oh, God," she said, "I've got to get over to the grand jury."

Larkin knew that ended their conversation. He gave up pressing her for more answers. He agreed that he'd count the bills and scribbled on a piece of typing paper, handing it over to her: "Attempted Bribe, offered to Court Reporter Lana Lewis, RPR," the way her name and title appeared on the envelope.

"Ms. Lewis," Larkin said, addressing her formally, trying to get the message across that he was pissed.

"Fuck me," she said, turning on her heels, walking out of his office; the clop, clop, clopping, going, then coming back into his office, tears rolling down her face.

"Thank you, Jay. Thank you."

"What are you going to tell Vince?" he asked.

"Nothing," she said, "I'm not going to tell him anything. He doesn't need another thing to worry about." Lana walked out toward Montage Street, and sprinted back across Court Street, with the traffic still backed up going over the Brooklyn Bridge.

CHAPTER 3

L arkin appeared paranoid observing the four corners of Chase, as if customers had overheard his conversation with Lana. Or he felt more inquisitive than paranoid to discover whatever he could with the little kernel Lana had shared with him.

Larkin spotted one of his banking clients, Lawrence Krone, a silver-headed criminal lawyer, who always appeared to have stepped out of a magazine ad for high-end suits and ties.

"How are you, Jay?" Krone asked as he stepped into the doorway of Larkin's office.

Jay flushed momentarily flipping hundred-dollar-bills face down.

"Up to my eyebrows in Ben Franklins," Larkin said, making it sound like more of a joke, not a strange thing for a banker to be sitting at his desk counting money.

Krone's stocky frame filled the doorway. He filled out his gray pinstriped suit and wasn't paying close attention to the bills spread out on Larkin's desk.

"Let me ask you a question," Larkin said, exploring the possibility of Krone's knowledge.

"Shoot," Krone said.

"Does the name Niccolo Giovanni ring a bell?" He let the name hang out there, then said nothing for fear of spilling the beans.

"Senior or Junior?" asked Krone. His question surprised Larkin.

"Can't say that I know. There's a father and son with the same name?"

"Yeah," Krone answered, poised to explain. "The poppa owns a popular Italian bakery on Van Brunt Street, across from the Brooklyn Army base. He also dabbles in illegal number and runs a betting parlor, all-night poker games, numbers racket right out of the building that houses the bakery. I guess you could say, the man shits where he eats."

Larkin listened intently, not uttering a sound or making a facial expression.

"Giovanni, the misses, and son live upstairs in a two-bedroom apartment. The Junior I've spoken about – they're originally from New Orleans, emigrated from Sicily a long time ago. His bakery business has been in Brooklyn more than ten, fifteen years now. Maybe more. I'm not sure."

Larkin waited for more information. Krone was eager to give it to him.

"He's not the kid's real father. He's the kid's godfather – stepfather kind of deal. The Senior married Agnes a long time ago; took her out of a convent, so it goes on the street. She had named the baby for him before they were even married. He had helped the girl when she was seventeen, maybe younger. Yep. The kid is known by Niccolo Giovanni, Junior."

Larkin looked interested and wanted to hear more of the story. He waited for Krone to continue. Krone took a swig of water out of the bottle he was holding.

"The son is a nice man, recently got himself jammed up and questioned by the police. They caught him carrying incriminating paper with numbers and names. The boy had no choice but to turn in his father."

Larkin stayed silent. He could never repeat what Lana had told him from what she had known working inside the grand jury.

"You don't have a problem with the son, do you?" Krone asked.

"No, no, nothing like that," Larkin said. "His name came up this morning. When I saw you, I figured you had connections with all the bad boys from Brooklyn."

Krone smiled. He accepted Larkin's remark as a compliment, as most defense attorneys might; they enjoyed having a strong rep defending the-not-so innocent-types.

Larkin was just about to say something when Krone cut him off.

"Hey, Jay, if you're having any trouble with any of these people, let me know. I admit they're small potatoes, but they do have "A Louie" on their payroll."

Larkin Looked puzzled. "What's 'A Louie'?"

Krone laughed. "Larkin, you don't know what "A Louie" is?"

Larkin shook his head.

"A wise guy, an enforcer. They call him Louie because that's kind of a tough street name. You know what I mean? 'Hey, I'll get Louie do to break your legs if you don't pay up.' That's how they use this guy. The bonus is it's the enforcer's last name. A goombah whose last name is L-E-W-I-S, Lewis. Different from Louie, but nevertheless he's a street tough. You know, a Joe Peche type."

That tidbit of information left Larkin reeling. Lana's last name was Lewis. She never used her married name, Scotto, ever.

Jay reinforced with Krone that he had no problems with either Giovanni and was just curious.

Krone feigned a salute and moved out of his Larkin's doorway and headed over to a teller's window.

****

The hundred-dollar notes that encompassed the "attempted bribe" Larkin recorded on paper that the bills weren't newly minted. Larkin checked to see if their numbers ran consecutively. They didn't.

This presented a conundrum for Larkin as he stacked the bills in $1,000 denominations. In front of him were fifteen piles of a thousand dollars each. He banded the bills in white paper, denoting the amount of $1,000 on the front. He slid the white envelope containing the bills into a larger brown interoffice envelope and wrote on the outside, $15,000.

Over the twenty years working in the banking industry, Larkin had counted more cash than the bribe money from an all-cash down payment from a Brooklyn rabbi for an apartment overlooking the Manhattan skyline from site of the promenade in Brooklyn Heights, not far from where the movie *Moon Struck* was filmed. He wasn't impressed by the $15,000 in cash.

Larkin swung around in his brown leather chair and unlocked the safe behind him. He placed the envelope containing the $15,000 on the first shelf, closed the door, spun the silver lock to the right and breathed a sigh of relief. Then he picked up the receiver of the phone on his desk and punched in numbers. The phone rang about three or four times, until an answering machine played this message: "Hello, this is the desk of Lana Lewis. If this is a transcript order, please call the clerk of the grand jury reporters at 718-624-3287. Leave your name and number with Silvia, and I'll be sure to get back to you as soon as possible. Thank you and have a nice day."

Larkin knew before he called he wasn't going to leave her a message. Nor was he going to call the grand jury clerk as suggested by Lana's phone message.

CHAPTER 4

Inside the dimly lit grand jury room, an NYPD police officer stood at the door as Lana's fingertips silently hit the keys of her black steno machine. The skill of reporting, introduced to Lana seven years earlier, taught her how to transform the machine's alphabet, phonetic symbols, into indelible ink on white brick-like paper. She had trained long and hard at court reporting school. And her confidence and determination made her stand out as one of the few women who had broken through the glass ceiling into a man's career.

With this type of stenography, the *machine writer*, the term often used in the field – reports, syllable by syllable, on all testimony. The black letters march across the page from left to right, with suffixes, the beginning sounds first, and the prefixes, on the left, as the ending sounds. The thumbs hit the vowel sounds, called *vocalizing*, which are the keys at the center bottom of the machine. With these twenty-four keys, Lana could write 225 wpm.

It's was such an automatic reflect, that has nothing to do with thinking, that most times Lana was off in another world while she was taking testimony. On this day, a day when she had run out of the office because of finding an envelope stacked with hundred-dollar-bills and a note that proclaimed, "take this money, lose your notes on the Giovanni indictment;" her mind drifted back to a simpler time, her childhood.

She remembered that at age six or seven she had been fascinated with inventing word games with her father. Something they had played for hours at the kitchen table, writing on slips of paper, long before Lana ever knew Scrabble was invented.

Costa had introduced his daughter into the world of exploring new words in with his very own torn paperback copy of Webster's Dictionary. This was the same dictionary he had carried with him on the journey from Italy to the United States as a teenager.

Costa and Lana loved playing word games together. These was years before Costa became a son of a bitch. It had happened overnight when Lana was 13 years old. That night Lana believed her father received a phone call from a woman. The caller identified herself as Costa's cousin when Lana answered the phone. The caller asked to speak to Costa and Lana handed her father the receiver. He had a strange look on his face. He stared at Lana while he spoke in Italian to the woman on the other end of the phone. Lana had heard him speak Italian with her mother and grandparents. But this woman's voice was not familiar. Two days later Costa didn't come home to their house in Hidden Pond. Soon after, Lana's mother found out that he had told his boss that he'd a family member had a stroke. Costa had said he needed to travel to New York City to help. His boss, the kitchen supervisor at a

Pennsylvania prison where Costa worked as a baker, gave him a week off.

As Lana took dictation inside the grand jury, her childhood memories plagued her. Her father's patience had wavered back then, which made her confused about her feelings for him. Two days after that phone call, he snapped at her and her mother. The phone call had made him nervous. She understood that. But then there were the times he had all the patience in the world to play word games with her. Lana loved those moments--learning new words, using them in sentences, writing them down in her journal. This is the same thing her father had done when he was a boy learning English.

Costa's voyage by steamer ship into the United States with his mother had been a daunting experience, he'd explained to his daughter. His emigration papers had been jumbled because he wasn't born in Italy but in Crete, when his father was serving in the military during the war.

"Being born on an island in Greece made me want to understand more and more about words. All words come from Greek roots," Costa had shared with his daughter.

He stressed how much he wanted her to learn more and more – there were things she had forgotten about her father that she had known she'd never get back.

She watched the paper flow into the tray of her machine, the black symbols drenched with ink. She couldn't all of it and that bothered her. It had something to do with the Greek letters and why colleges had chapters of Greek societies. The great men of Greece he encouraged her to read, but she never had. Once he left, her mother had no time for her. She remembered wandering through the complex of Hidden Pond – and one day she had become a superhero.

Lana had sat at her kitchen table – playing with crayons – coloring, making shapes when she heard a woman scream. Her mother was in the basement washing clothes. Lana ran outside in the cold, without wearing a coat. A woman stood at the edge of the icy pond where the kids skated when it was thick enough. The pine trees were glazed over with frost – but the sun was warm like a spring day.

The woman was still screaming when Lana got to her side of the pond. The woman's puppy had fallen through the ice. Lana did not think. She kicked off her slippers and in her pink OMarie-Elaina, pajamas she waded into the frozen pond, and with her tiny fingers, grabbed on to the dog's collar and pulled him into her arms. By that time, her mother was screaming. "h, my God, Lana's going to drown."

But Lana hadn't drowned. Inside herself knew she wouldn't drown. She saved the dog's life. The woman was crying, holding on to her frozen puppy. Lana wanted to pet it, but her mother pulled her inside her coat and took her daughter away from the scene that had now filled with many people who had come out of their houses.

"Why did you do that? Didn't you realize you could have drowned?"

"I wasn't worried," she had said to her mother in between her teeth chattering."

It was that determination that she needed to draw upon now. She reminded herself that she wouldn't let anyone scare her into a situation ever again. She was no longer a child, but a mother of two grown daughters. She would not be afraid of someone who feared coming out in the open to see her face-to-face. She believed in herself. She could do anything she would set her mind to.

In her mind's eye, she had a clear picture of her father sitting at their Formica kitchen table, thumbing through the dictionary. He had inspired her.

"Look up words. Learn how to spell them. Understand their meanings. You'll never go wrong. You'll be able to talk to doctors, lawyers and judges one day," he had told her, never realizing the truth of his statement.

Little did Costa know that his daughter, the young teenager he had abandoned, would go on to a career in law enforcement within the judicial system.

"Little Superhero Lana braved cold and icy pond water to save Mrs. Samuel's pup Jennie. The ten-year old kicked off her fuzzy slippers and waded into the pond, keeping her head above the icy depths, that had broken off, where she spotted Jennie and lifted her to safety."

CHAPTER 5

S till deep in thought, Lana never heard, Assistant District Attorney Sara Bronson calling a morning recess.

"Lana! Hello, Ms. Lewis, are you with us? We're done for this morning." Lana remained comatose, her mind somewhere back in Pennsylvania, approximately three decades ago. She hadn't heard a word the assistant district attorney had said. Her fingers kept striking the little blank keys.

"Lana!" Bronson yelled. Lana's head shot up, startled.

"Are you all right?"

"I'm sorry," Lana muttered. "I guess I've been deep in thought."

"You certainly were somewhere else. Not here. But your fingers were going at their usual quick pace. You've piqued my curiosity. Look at your notes."

Lana pulled up the last couple of folds from the paper tray. She stared at the symbols, reading aloud what she had written.

"I wrote that you were calling my name, trying to get my attention. You said, 'Lana, we're done for this morning.'" Then she blushed.

"Well, I'm glad your fingers are still alert, even when your mind isn't in the room."

Lana remarked, "One thing about my fingers. They never quit even when my brain does."

"Glad to hear that," Bronson said, confused but not concerned in the least.

Bronson watched as Lana pushed the stack of paper back inside the tray that fit inside the body of the machine.

"See you this afternoon," Lana called to Bronson, as she walked out the door from the grand jury room.

Bronson yelled back, "Enjoy your lunch. We won't start back today until 2:30. I'm attempting to finish up the Gutierrez case this afternoon. Maybe you can get home early and get some rest. You look like you need it."

Rest, Lana thought. What's that? She exited the Supreme Court building from the side door on Adams Street, and traversed the park. Her stomach gurgled on empty while other court personnel were seated on the steps in the sunshine eating their lunches. The noontime whistle blew and Lana continued her walk knowing she had plenty of time.

As she strolled towards the Court Street side of the building, she saw something flash in her peripheral vision; an object above her head. She turned her attention to the pigeons and birds hovering above an old woman's head. The woman was throwing cube-sized pieces of bread.

The shabbily dressed bag lady wore a stained apron over a much dirtier dress. She reminded Lana of her grandmother, Genevieve, when she had gotten too old to care. Instinctively, Lana moved closer to the woman, then stopped, realizing her eyes had played tricks on her. Her grandmother had been dead twenty years. She dismissed the idea that this woman looked anything like her grandmother.

She chalked her impulsive nature telling herself it had been a strange day. A bribe, memories of the past coming back to haunt her. It could be possible her mother and grandmother were sending her a warning. They had always guarded and protected her.

She promised herself before the day was over, she'd go over to Saint Anne's and light a candle.

Inside the lobby, a bride and groom held the door of the elevator open for Lana. She quickened her pace and squeezed inside the door as it was about to close. The couple looked too young and cute to be getting married.

The bride had on a light blue dress and the groom's tuxedo matched her ensemble. He had a white carnation pinned to his lapel, and she had a bouquet of white and dyed blue carnations wrapped in white satin. Just the two of them. No family. No friends.

"Congratulations," Lana said extending her hand to the groom. "You look too young to be getting married."

"We're not that young," the bride laughed, pressing the second-floor button. "I'm turning twenty in a couple of months." "Oh, my," Lana's face flushed. She thought the girl wasn't older than sixteen. "I guess I'm the one getting old," she said. "When you start to think cops and people getting married look like teenagers, that's when you know, it's you who's getting older."

They couple laughed at Lana's expense.

They exited the floor where the Justice of the Peace held weddings for the City of New York. Lana continued her ride up to the third floor. Most of the cubicles were empty. There were one or two typists plugged in to recording devices, typing transcripts, listening to dictation.

Lana sat at her desk behind the square glassed-in office. She printed her name on a blank piece of paper in her supervisor's log. The vacationing Rob Smith, the person in charge of homicide and grand jury reporters, the person Lana knew she needed to report the bribe to, wouldn't be back until Monday. And this was only Friday. Monday seemed years away

CHAPTER 6

Later that afternoon, Lana went back through the park, toward the courthouse that housed the grand jury rooms.

Lana's stomach growled despite filling her tummy with sugary Coca Cola, hoping that it would aid the nausea coming up her throat. She slowly sipped the can of Coke through a straw sitting outside on a bench in front of the courthouse, hoping the feeling would pass.

Inside the grand jury room, jurors gathered. A flurry of questions about Lana were being posed to ADA Bronson.

One of the male jurors asked if the ADA could find out if Lana was okay. Another juror had whispered to Bronson that Lana looked flush like she was running a fever. When a female juror reported seeing Lana run past her into the ladies' room, Bronson had agreed she'd find out, saying, she was also a bit concerned herself about Lana.

When Lana arrived back inside the grand jury room, where the windows were wide open, blowing in bus fumes from the bottled up-traffic outside, Lana paled in comparison to how she had appeared in the morning session.

"Hi! Are you feeling all right?" Lana stared up at Bronson, surprised.

"Several jurors are concerned about you. They are asking me to ask you if you're okay." Lana said, "Really?" She was touched.

"I had some stomach problems earlier this morning. I'm feeling much better now." Bronson didn't want to ask the obvious question if Lana was pregnant.

"I'm glad," she said. "Go thank the jurors. They were worried about you."

"Of course, I will. Thank you." Lana approached the wooden railing, the bar that separated the jurors from the center of the courtroom.

"Thank you, guys, for asking about me. You guys are the best. I'm actually feeling better this afternoon." After a brief chat with the jurors, Lana went back to her machine and took her seat.

ADA Bronson didn't want to ask Lana the obvious question: are you pregnant.

******

"Jurors, may I have your attention," ADA Bronson announced. "We are moving forward with this afternoon's calendar, Part 2 of the Gutierrez case."

The female prosecutor picked up the grand jury's monthly calendar to remind herself that this panel of jurors has one more week to serve on the jury.

"Your service as grand jurors terminates at the end of next week. This case must be voted on this afternoon. I am asking all, including Ms. Lewis, to stay behind a few minutes extra, if we haven't voted by five o'clock."

She signaled to the police officer at the front door to bring Gutierrez in from the hallway.

"Mr. Gutierrez will be giving you his testimony. It is important that you keep in mind that the indictment for second-degree murder charges have now been reduced to manslaughter. After we hear the witness's testimony, I will charge you on the relevant law as it applies to these new charges at the end of the hearing."

Lana reported the instructional words Bronson had said to the jurors, plus she prepared herself for what might turn out to be fast-paced questions and answers, like a tennis match at Forest Hills. Lana always carried along a pocket-sized recording device in case words went flying in the air. If she found herself in trouble, she'd turn it on. It would aid her in transcribing the testimony later.

She whispered a little prayer to herself that her mind wouldn't wonder on this one. She wondered how many court reporters would have showed up and worked after receiving a bribe. She hadn't a care in the world five hours earlier. Now, all she thought about was the name Niccolo Giovanni.

Juan Gutierrez, who had been escorted into the grand jury room by a NYPD officer, was asked to take the stand. Gutierrez was a thin Hispanic fellow of about thirty-years old. He had dark facial hair, a cleanly shaven head and tattoos on the knuckles of his hands.

Lana approached Gutierrez.

"Please place your right hand on the bible and raise your left hand."

The witness followed her instruction. She noticed the tattooed word on his right hand said FAMILY. She looked over at his raised left hand, it said GOD

Lana recited the oath: "Do you swear to tell the truth, the whole truth in the matter of The State of New York vs. Juan Gutierrez; and nothing but the truth, so help you God?"

Gutierrez answered, "Yes, I do,"

Lana's skin crawled after repeating the words of the oath. She immediately visualized her father's features in her head, his big head of curly hair; she wondered if there was now any gray strands running through his chestnut hair. If Costa were sitting in the courtroom, he might be shocked seeing his daughter in a position of authority, especially asking a witness to swear to tell the truth.

Costa had never trusted Lana after he had caught her in telling lies over the years that they had lived together. He would find this remarkable; in her duties as a court stenographer she repeated the oath to a witness.

***

The Gutierrez case had bothered Lana from the first day she had taken a previous eye-witnesses to the crime. As she now observed the Hispanic young man who had been accused of murdering his younger brother – this case would have bothered anyone listening. It had all the earmarks of a crime committed out of hatred. Yet, there hung in the balance an element of truth – that this was not an intentional act of an older brother against a younger brother.

While this man's attorney was allowed in the room to observe his client being questioned, he was permitted to interact with the jury on behalf of his client. But if his client felt the need to speak with his attorney, that would be allowed in private.

Gutierrez's face looked tortured and pale against the darker skin on the rest of his body. Stress lines had formed in the corners of his bloodshot eyes; they ran upward like a woman's eye makeup. It also appeared that he hadn't slept in days.

Lana searched his face, noticed his overall body language, noticed that he had lost a significant amount of weight since the case had first came into the grand jury several weeks ago. While Gutierrez claimed responsibility for his younger brother's death, he pled it was not an intentional murder.

Something about the case affected Lana to her core.

Gutierrez sat in the witness box. The jurors put their newspapers and magazines aside. They focused their attention on the young man in the hot seat.

Lana's fingers hovered above the keyboard as Bronson spoke. She asked the witness to state his name and address, and she reminded him that he was still under oath from testifying once before in this case.

"I am going to re-ask questions, Mr. Gutierrez, to refresh the jurors' recollection taking them back to the day of your niece Angelica's christening."

Gutierrez spoke, attempting to refresh the jurors' recollection. "The argument happened after the baby's baptism. We were finished in church. Friends and family were picking up their belongings from the pews and walking down the center aisle of the church to the foyer and out the old wooden doors of the church."

"Tell the jurors when the actual argument broke out between you and Jesus."

"Originally, I was teasing him. We hadn't had an argument. I was just breaking his balls, you know -- mocking him because he had become a father so young, seventeen, you know, he was not even shaving yet. It was just my way of reminding my younger brother how much harder he'd have to work now to buy formula and diapers. Then I started on stuff like getting up in the middle of the night. That's when I saw a sour angry expression on his face. He scowled at me because he had taken offense to my teasing. Jesus doesn't like getting up early in the mornings. He became defensive, me calling him out.

I didn't like him saying, 'Oh, big man, Bro. You're the big man now 'cause you have a steady job.' I didn't say another word. I could see his face flush; he was embarrassed."

Bronson stayed silent, waited and watched the witness formulating his words.

"I don't know where it came from, but Jesus starts yelling, He tells me to stop staring at his wife. I swear I wasn't staring at her. He just wanted to start something. He babbled about something that I had said years ago that his wife was a whore. I don't even know where that came from. I might have said it when they had first started dating. Jeez, you know, Ma'am, we were at his kid's baptism. Jesus got louder, hostile towards me. He pushed me, and I fell down two concrete steps outside the church, saying I better not come to the baby's party."

Gutierrez searched the faces of the jurors who were listening attentively. "I swear," he said looking at the jurors. "I don't even remember taking the penknife out of my pocket."

"Mr. Gutierrez, was it your intention to kill your brother, Jesus, on that day outside of Saint Mary's Star of the Sea Catholic Church?"

"Never! I never meant to do anything like that. It was his baby's christening. When he turned his back on me and said I shouldn't go to the baby's party, he like turned his back on me, walked away. I pulled out the small blade from my pocket and jabbed it in his ass, just to get his attention. I didn't mean for it to sever an artery. It was an accident."

Gutierrez shrugged his boney shoulders beneath his wrinkled dress shirt and crookedly knotted tie.

He repeated, "It was an accident." He stared into the faces of the jurors, pleading with them for mercy. "I didn't mean to kill my brother," his voice cracked, tears flowed down his cheeks, making water marks on his blue shirt.

Bronson raised her hand, held up the proceeding, allowing Gutierrez to catch his breath. He put up his hands to cover his face and wept loud gut-wrenching, uncontrollable sobs.

Gutierrez's pain coursed through Lana's body. So many times, as a child, she had sobbed in the very same way, never understanding why her father tortured her. Always accusing her of sticking up for her mother. They were hurtful times in Lana's life that had come back to haunt as she worked in courtrooms on other people's crimes.

She had prayed for this witness since the first time his case came before the grand jurors, which allowed her to find out something about herself: This might be her avocation in life to pray for all the defendants whose cases she worked on. She understood their pain from her own life.

Her thoughts went further back to her childhood, as Gutierrez tried to control his emotions.

She remembered she was ten years old and had snuck her father's lighter into her pocket, taking it from the dining room table. She had taken it with her into the bathroom. Her head pounded, thinking of the house on Hidden Pond. It had been a lonely place where she had no allies, no grandma to love and protect her. It had been the place where her mother and father constantly fought. She had believed for a long time now that her father left her mother because of her.

Lana's chest tightened as one of the jurors handed Ms. Bronson a soft package of tissues for Gutierrez to dry his face.

As much as Lana wanted to stop thinking about that day she had spun the wheel of a Zippo lighter, the mind pictures wouldn't go away. The visual in her head, she saw herself press the wheel of the lighter with her tiny finger.

With every pause in the questioning, Gutierrez blew his nose and wiped his eyes, Lana remembered having that lighter in her hands, flipping it open, spinning the wheel, witnessing red and blue sparks appear from nowhere. She knew if she pushed harder the next time, she'd be able to get it lit.

Again, her little fingers tried harder to ignite a fire. Then panicked when the orange-blue flame appeared in her hands.

Gutierrez composed himself. How had this baby's christening made him so revengeful? It was supposed to be a happy occasion. He remembered pulling the penknife's pearl handle from his pocket, pretending it was as big as a sword. "How can you hurt someone with a knife this small?" he asked, spreading his fingers to show the size.

Lana wrote the word on her machine "indicating" surrounding it in parenthesis, on the paper that flowed through the roller of her machine, as the witness spread his thumb and index finger an inch apart.

Bronson asked more questions of the witness. Lana's fingers fell into the smooth syncopation like that of a metronome. The back and forth of the words became mesmerizing. Bronson paused from the witness and spoke to the jurors as to their role in the case.

Lana thought about her own crimes, not so much about the fire in the bathroom, but the lies she had told to protect herself. When she looked down at the paper flowing through the roller of her machine, each phonetic sound of the words appeared creating the exchange between Bronson and Gutierrez; the exchange between Bronson and the jurors; it was all written there on her reporter's paper.

Sometimes she amazed herself that even while her mind was off in Hidden Pond, her fingers automatically listened.

Ten-year-old Lana never remembered smelling smoke after she had ignited the roll of toilet paper in her parents' bathroom. But she had remembered the smell of the lighter fluid, something so keen an aroma, as she placed the lighter's flame under a square of toilet paper that had hang down blowing in the air. In an instant, flames had blurred her vision.

Anger had blurred Gutierrez's vision.

"My brother turned his back, walked away from me. 'No, man.' I said, "No, Bro, you don't get away with that.'" He looked directly at the jurors as his face quivered. "I know I did this, but I didn't mean to kill my brother."

As the toilet paper raged in Lana's parents' bathroom, the same tiny hands that lit the fire grabbed roll of dry toilet paper. As flames had grown larger, Lana risked burning her hands, and push the paper into the water of the toilet bowel. She closed the lid and flushed the evidence away. At least that's what she had thought at the time.

CHAPTER 7

After the jurors voted that Juan Gutierrez would now be arraigned, bail would be set to allow him freedom until his case was transferred to the Criminal Court.

Lana left the courtroom feeling exhausted. She had amazed herself that she had been able to work the entire day. Thinking about the bribe scared her; she tried as hard as she could to put it out of her mind.

She thanked Larkin in a silent prayer, who she had started to think about as her Guardian Angel. He had exonerated her from carrying all that money in her purse riding on the subway. Walking into the subway station, she rubbed her empty stomach and looked for a vending machine to purchase Ginger Ale. Before she had taken change out of her pocket, she suddenly hunched over, gagging as she had earlier in the ladies' bathroom.

She walked to the end of the dank station into a dingy bathroom where the foul smell of urine made her feel worse. She enclosed herself in a tacky looking at the foul language displayed on the wall.

She took a wad of toilet paper and pressed the scratchy paper against her mouth. Even with the filth that surrounded her, she wasn't ready to get on a train and ride the subway home.

She covered the seat sufficiently and sat on the bowl. Her body eliminated whatever poison it had held in for most of the day. She had remembered the evening before eating cold pizza Vince had left her in the refrigerator. But she had done that many times before.

Her body shook all over like some vicious virus had taken over every cell in her being. *Could this be stress*, she wondered? She had hated putting Larkin in a situation but couldn't help herself.

Maybe it was Gutierrez crying like a baby that made her feel so sick? She felt feverish, hot and cold, at the same time; her stomach spasmed. Then a thought popped into her head. *Could I be pregnant?*

CHAPTER 8

S even o'clock that night, Lana heard a key turn in the front door. Vince came into the house wondering why every light had been turned on.

"Hon, why is every light on?"

Lana tried lifting her lids open. She couldn't remember how long she had been lying on the couch. She tried to prop herself up on a pillow to answer him. Her head felt too heavy to lift.

Vince had removed his shoes and stepped quietly into the den looking at Lana on the gray plush couch. He automatically placed his hand to her forehead when he saw her face flush.

"Hey, what's going on?" he asked. She stirred, just didn't wake.

He took another look at his wife bundled in a winter bathrobe, walked into the kitchen where the windows over the sink faced their backyard. He ran sink, wet a dish towel with cold water and poured Lana a glass of water. He removed a surgical mask from the cabinet above and slipped it over his mouth and nose. He brought a glass of water to her.

In a soothing voice, he whispered, "Hon, Lana?" She looked up at him through slits in her eyes. She saw Vince wearing a blue hospital mask and wondered *why am I in the hospital?*

"Have you taken any aspirin?" He asked. "You're on fire."

"No," she responded, opening her eyes and quickly closing them.

This time Vince went through the hallway and up the steps to their bedroom. He removed two Advil from the medicine chest, climbed back down to the den. He coaxed Lana to sit up and open her mouth.

"Swallow these," he said. He put the tablets on her tongue and handed her the glass of water.

*****

During the night going into the next morning, Lana felt Vince touch her while she remained sleeping on the couch.

She found herself in an old Fiat they used to own, driving the car through the Brooklyn Battery Tunnel; her eyes teary from gas fumes, coming up from an opening on the floor. She stepped on the gas to get out of the tunnel faster, pushing the pedal down. The car moved ten miles an hour.

A tinge of pollution hung in the atmosphere outside the tunnel. She sped through lower Manhattan. She prayed she wouldn't vomit. She couldn't get sick now. Vince needed her to pick him up at Saint Vincent's at 4 o'clock. He'd be outside waiting in the cold if she was late. He could get sick. She hit the gas pedal, the car lurched. She was passing the Twin Towers. A few more blocks to go. She stopped at a red light and looked up at the Towers twinkling in the sky.

*****

Early Friday morning, Lana heard a car backing out of their driveway. It was Vince leaving for work. She found a note from on her pillow, letting her know that he had gone to his office. The note prompted her to look at a snack table he had set up in front of her with orange juice and two more Advil. She ran into the bathroom – she hadn't gone all night.

By Friday afternoon Lana still felt a bit foggy but still totally recalled Wednesday and all that had happened.

I'm ill, she realized. *Not bribe sick, but sick sick. Like flu sick.*

She padded out of the bathroom recalling being in Jay's office. The entire event played in her head. Oh, the subway station, after she had wretched, she had boarded the train, and thought an older man with silver hair reading the *Progresso*, an Italian newspaper, kept watching her. He had lifted his eyes several times and stared at her. She feared he might come and sit next to her. Maybe he was the one who had left the envelope on her desk that morning.

She considered the possibility. Then it was possible the man was following her home. She thought she'd throw up the orange juice she had just drunk. She laid her head back down the pillow and slept some more.

Driving the car again into Manhattan, she had stopped at a red light, and saw green and red lights twinkling from the Twin Towers. She felt stuck in some scary dream. The kind people have when they are hallucinating.

*****

It wasn't until Saturday morning when Lana realized that she had lost three days of her life. It made her believe her illness was fortuitous because Vince had never questioned her about working her supervisor's shift. Rob Smith, who had taken an extra three days off for an extended weekend.

Several hours later, clarity was eventually restored. Wednesday morning unfolded like a film playing in her mind, running down the steps and out into the street to Chase Bank. That's when Jay had gotten angry with her.

Recalling the afternoon grand jury, the Gutierrez indictment. Getting to the subway station later than usual; the platform empty from the usual suspects, people she would have said hello to. Trying to resolve the film that played over and over in her head. That's when Lana smelled chicken soup and realized she was hungry. She went into the hallway bathroom to wash up, with the aroma of soup wafting under her nose.

"Oh, my God!" Lana said, looking at herself in the mirror above the sink. Sticky strands of hair were glued against her face. She opened a jar of Noxzema, lifted a glob and swirled it over her face. She brushed her teeth, using her hands as a cup to rinse her mouth.

She slipped her arms from the pink robe that she had been wearing for three days and walked slowly towards the kitchen. Vince was stirring a pot of chicken soup.

"Hey, how are my daughters?" she asked.

Vince turned quickly, smiling and happy to see her standing on her feet.

"She speaks," he joked. "And she walks, too." Vince gave her a full blow-by-blow on their daughters. He slid a chair away from the countertop and urged Lana to sit.

Steam rose from the pot, and Vince spooned soup into a bowl. Lana stirred the chicken and noodles round and round, trying to cool it off.

Vince poured soup for himself into a mug.

"Jackie looked terrific," he said. Vince had always found a way to praise his 'mini-me'. "She's got herself a cute haircut. Tapered on the right side, accentuating those great cheekbones. Boy, is she one hell of a beauty." Jackie was his favorite.

"And Megan?" Lana asked, while Vince sipped soup from a mug with Santa's face on it.

"Megan is Megan." he said. "A sassy little bitch just like her mother. All work, no play." Lana rolled her eyebrows. Not that Vince noticed. She'd let the comment go, sort of glad she hadn't told him what had taken place with her in her office on Wednesday morning.

Lana gathered scratched up chicken and noodles from the bottom of her bowl and placed it in her mouth. She wanted more but didn't ask.

She had wanted to tell Vince everything, believed that she should before the situation worsened. Wives are supposed to tell their husbands. Wasn't it her obligation? Mandatory even?

Her eyes followed the leaves swaying in the backyard through the glass patio door. She admired the birds, free to go wherever they wanted, in and out of the willow tree. She thought of something to ask him.

"Tell me about their new apartment."

"It's perfect. One bedroom on campus, which I'm really pleased about," Vince said. "I didn't like their first choice, the downtown area. Too far from campus. I hated thinking of them driving on icy roads back and forth to class. I definitely feel better now that they can walk from their apartment to classes when it snows."

"Was it clean?' Lana asked, never really knowing what Vince might think was perfect.

"The bathroom needed a new toilet seat, and some cabinet paper, a shade on the window. We'd shopped for that. They even bought nice curtains that we hung on the kitchen window to insure their privacy."

Vince couldn't hold out a second longer now he saw the color coming back into Lana's cheeks.

"Hey, who did you get to fill in for Rob? I'm guessing you haven't been back to the office since Wednesday."

"Jolie was happy to do it. I swapped days with her. I'm going in this Monday on my day off to make it up to her."

"Grand Jury busy?" he asked.

"Always," she said, not looking in his direction, not adding anything about Gutierrez case being completed – not that Vince would ever had asked her for grand jury information. But he had known about the case going to the grand jury since the change of indictment had hit the newspapers.

"Term ends next week," Vince said.

"Yes, I'll be happy to have the girls back home for a little while." she answered.

"No, not the term at Binghamton. I meant your grand jurors, the turnover."

"Oh, grand jury," she said. "Yep this one's over in another week."

Did that made her feel any better knowing Giovanni's case might go over to be voted on by a different jury? Not with her being the court reporter of record.

CHAPTER 9

Bright and early Monday morning, Lana, thought it best to wear a pair of white sneakers with her cream-colored suit. Anyone who knew her would see the sneakers and know she was completely and utterly exhausted.

After cleaning off the black tar that had stuck to her heels from melting asphalt in the crosswalk, she instinctively knew she'd never be able to walk twice that day from the DA's office back to the Supreme Court building in four-inch heels.

She had noted some things in her journal, marking last Wednesday to today, as the "week from hell." Her tummy still felt in flutters and she wasn't a hundred percent sure she had kicked whatever the bug was.

But as a perfectionist, Lana made it her business to focus on the issues that were now ahead of her. First, having to tell her supervisor why she had been absent on Thursday and Friday. That would have to be followed by the more important topic -- that she had received a bribe and that she hadn't told anyone in the DA's office about it.

She also needed to borrow Rob's keys to allow her access to her June 6th notes, on the said indictment of Niccolo

Giovanni. She prompted herself to avoid the word stolen. Then she had to come up how to explain the entire June 16 episode, how she'd asked Jolie to replace her and why she had handed the bribe money over to Larkin.

Larkin! She then remembered placing a phone call to him while she was home sick, promising that she would not hesitate to report what had happened the first thing on Monday morning to her supervisor.

She also recalled she had spoken to Jolie, who had been kind enough to cover for her and Bob Smith on Thursday and Friday. The pieces were piecing themselves together like a puzzle, shifting around in her head.

"Please help me get through this," Lana asked Jolie over the phone. "There was a man tonight," she said.

"What man are you talking about?" Jolie asked.

"Sitting across from me on the subway. He kept staring up from his newspaper, kept looking at me. If I didn't feel so sick." She had cut her own words off. "I'd swear I had seen him in our building yesterday. I'm so confused. Could I be imagining all of this?"

Lana had to trust someone. She needed to know what her friend would do if she was in her situation. She also wanted her to know that if something happened to her, like turning up kidnapped, or dead, murdered and left somewhere to rot, at least Jolie would have some of the information.

"I need you to cover for me for the next two days. I'm positive I'll get better if I stay home and rest. Jolie, I'm afraid to go to the office right now. At least until Vince comes back."

"Of course, I'll switch with you," Jolie had said, allowing Lana to breathe in a sigh of relief.

Now that Jolie and Larkin were aware of Lana's whereabouts, she'd be able to rest knowing that she wouldn't have to think about anything until Monday.

Lana believed that she had good instincts. She also believed she wasn't working inside the grand jury for nothing. Her notetaking skill was also for her safety and that of her daughters. She understood nice people didn't use bribes as a form of communicating. She had finally wrapped her head around those circumstances, and like Jolie, she needed to call upon her instincts.

While Pennsylvania country-born Jolie Wilson, acted like a city-slicker, she had coached Lana during their phone conversation, "Talk to him, girlfriend. You can trust Rob Smith to know the right thing to do. He's always been the kind of man that stands behind his reporters."

Lana churned Jolie's idea over and over in her head about talking with Rob. She still wasn't as confident as she'd like to have been. Had this ever even happened to a court reporter before? She asked Jolie that question.

Jolie admitted she didn't know the answer. Neither she nor Lana had ever heard of anyone working in the grand jury or as a homicide steno for DA's office having ever being offered a bribe.

Rumors floated around about attorneys who had been approached by a person of interest. Attorneys knew better to never talk to a court reporter, even if they wanted to order a copy of the transcript, which they couldn't have from a grand jury testimony, just from homicide. It had come out as a joke. Something like, "You know, Ms. Reporter, you don't have to rush that transcript on my account." Sure, this attorney, fully cognizant that he had broken a rule of ethics, just in talking to a grand jury reporter.

While lawyers enjoyed having their day in court, if a transcript was going to reveal something negative towards their client, they'd ask – or joke might be the right word.

Lana had often mentioned to Vince, in the privacy of their home, that she had, with her own eyes and ears, spotted deals going down in the hallway of the courthouse involving prosecutors and defense attorneys. Not that that's rare. That's how plea bargains are struck.

*****

Lana thought about the sleazy attorneys and her mind went immediately to her father.

Costa had his set of lapsed morals, almost like the criminals who had disgusted her over the years. The crimes they had committed against other human beings – wasn't it so with her father, abandoning his own wife and child? Leaving them in a strange town? While Lana's pea brain couldn't remember the exact moment of her father's departure, she had remembered her mother not shedding one single tear. Lana had always wondered if her mother was being brave for her sake.

****

One afternoon, while she was alone, after her mother had gone out to work, Lana recalled sneaking into her parents' room, sliding open their clothes closet doors and instantly smelling her father's presence. His aftershave which lingered long after he had gone.

She didn't know the brand. But the fragrance had longevity, still popular in the 1990s, and the aroma lingered long after a man had passed her in the hallway or stood next to her on the train. The scent had always reminded her of her father, bringing her to a time in her life when she felt inferior and hadn't understood why.

Her father had been a handsome devil. Always manicured, clean, his dark curly hair, thick and healthy. He was wearing a navy-blue pea coat, the one with the big round black buttons, the day he had left for work and never come back home again.

Her mother had never bothered calling the police or listing him as a missing person. Maria had known all along. There had always been another woman in Costa's life. Although, he had hidden his betrayal well, there were clues along the way.

While Lana had laid in a feeling of suspended animation on her couch for five days, she had pictured the day when she had traveled with her mother by bus to an Italian neighborhood in Brooklyn. She believed then, as she did now, that Maria was looking for someone. But Lana hadn't known who.

She had observed her mother spying into store windows, the kind of stores that hung sausage and balls of provolone cheese in the windows. The purple emblem embossed on the hunks of cheese with the word Italy imprinted.

They were called pork stores. Or *Salumaria*, as these stores were called in Italian. Businesses where Maria walked inside and confronted whoever was working behind the counter with a barrage questions.

Lana hadn't known who she was looking for at that time. But it must have been where Maria and Costa had first lived and opened a bakery before moving on to Pennsylvania.

Grandma Jennie had lived in that neighborhood a long time ago, after her mother and father had gotten married and everyone moved to Brooklyn from New Orleans.

CHAPTER 10

O n Monday morning, Lana walked through the corridor into her office at the District Attorney's office. She spotted Rob immediately. The office lights cast a shine on the top of his head, that was bent over, as he sorted through paperwork. The fluffy light brown hair, surrounding a small bald spot, had gotten scarcer.

The courage Lana had mustered up earlier had drifted away like a fine mist over the ocean. She had promised Larkin and Joline that she wouldn't hesitate one minute to tell the truth, jump right in and admit...what? It wasn't a crime, was it, to have taken the money and note to Larkin? Lana's bravado vanished like April snow on a sunny day.

She knew, sooner or later, she'd have to say good morning to her boss, so she faked coughed. Rob turned his head and faced her.

"Hey, just the girl I wanted to see." He got up and approached her, opening his arms, giving her a hug.

"I heard about you," he said.

Heard what? Joline couldn't have told him. Could she?

"So how are you feeling?" he asked. Oh! That! She pulled herself together and faked a smile.

"I can't believe how sick I was," she said, staring into his baby blues. "I'm better. Much better, in fact. Who told you?"

"I assumed it wasn't a secret. Vince told me. He said you didn't know what day of the week it was or where you were. How the hell did you get so sick? I mean, kind of strange for summer, don't you think?"

Vince was the culprit. She had guessed he had tried to pave the way for her before returning to the office, and he must have called Rob, divulging her illness.

She and Rob sat on leather chairs at his desk. He chatted about vacation, the weekend cruise he and his wife had taken.

She stared up at the clock on the wall. She had five minutes to pack supplies and walk over to the grand jury as Joline's substitute. That's when she realized she didn't have keys to unlock her desk drawer.

"Hey, Rob, my keys went missing," she said. "They weren't in my correspondence box when I came to work on Wednesday. Did you happen to pick them up?"

Rob went over to his desk and pulled out a bunch of keys on a tarnished circular ring. He looked through the bunch.

"No. I don't have yours. Take mine for now."

She took the keys, thanked him, and walked back to her desk where she unlocked her drawer. When the drawer opened, she quickly scanned the dates on the top of the notes. She removed June 6, 1999, the date mentioned in the bribe note, stuck the whole pack wrapped with the names of the day's defendants, picked up a supply of steno pads and locked the drawer.

Rob had gone back to sitting at his desk; head bent over scanning his logbook.

In a low voice, that she couldn't even hear herself, she whispered.

"Think we can have lunch together this afternoon?" He turned and faced her, surprised by her request.

"Something wrong?" he asked. She shook her head.

"I need to talk to you but I'm working for Joline, can't do it now." He saw she was nervous.

He said, "Sure. My office?" She nodded her head and walked into the corridor and stood near the elevator.

Rob walked out after her, curious about what had happened while he was out of the office on vacation, "What do you want to eat?" he asked, scrutinizing her expression.

"Let's share something," she said. "My stomach is still on the fritz," she said. "Ginger Ale would be nice."

Lana noticed he was wearing a blue blazer with brass buttons, something she had never seen him wear before. Rob was a suit man. He never wore blazers or sports coats. He seemed younger somehow. He looked Brooks Brothers.

"I like your outfit," she said, "Very Captain and Teneal."

He laughed, stretching out his arms, showing off the blazer. "Have a good morning," he said. "Try steering clear of the bad guys." He smirked his usual grin of approval at her. She could honestly say she loved the man. He had been so great to her from day they met. There was no click-clopping on the marble floor. Because Lana had never changed out of sneakers into her high heels.

Out of all those Lana had ever met in their industry, from other stenographers, to detectives and supervisors, Rob was the most compassionate. He had been there for her when her mother died and allowed her time to settle her mom's affairs. She believed with her whole heart that she would feel a lot better once she had told him about the events of last Wednesday.

It wasn't unheard of for a reporter to misplace notes. If that's the direction she had decided to go in. Rob had instilled in all his reporters an accountability method against losing notes: wrapping the dated calendars around the chunk of paper. He had constantly stressed to his staff that they should work on transcription end of the job way before the due date, which was usually thirty days from the date the hearing was held.

He showed every new-bee how to fix a hole in a transcript in case they had dropped a word or more. He knew the entire legal arena, the prosecutors' scripts, and the charges they had prepared and would ultimately read for the grand jurors before voting on an indictment.

Sometimes it happened that a reporter couldn't read his or her own chicken scratch, faint outlines, missing suffix or prefix. Reporters, after all, were human beings, not machines; they worked the magic machine, but they were not infallible, as much as judges and lawyers believed otherwise.

Walking through Pigeon Park to the Supreme Court, Lana treaded easier. Even her case felt lighter. Maybe by the end of the day, her soul might be lighter too.

*****

The standard lunch hour was twelve-thirty to one p.m., according to the discernment of the prosecutor presenting grand jury cases.

At the lunch break, Lana walked back through the park to the District Attorney's office, hopped on the elevator and arrived in Rob's office ten minutes later. She made it a point not to stop and say hello to any of the typists or other stenographers.

Rob had a can Ginger Ale on his desk, and he had cut a bagel, smeared with yellow mustard over turkey, waiting on a white paper plate for Lana. He pointed at half a pickle. She shook her head. He put the pickle on his plate.

Without any prompting, or small talk about his vacation, or the usual BS, or reiterating how sharp he looked in his captain's blazer, or who had just docked the Queen Mary in Red Hook, Lana launched right into it. She sat across from him and let in all spill out. At the end of the story, she even admitted that was an idiot for going to the bank and seducing Larkin

into holding the bribe money.

"I can't exaggerate how many hundred-dollar bills were stuffed inside the envelope. It had to have been at least ten thousand dollars." She continued to lay out the details of why she confided in Larkin. She said everything she had wanted to say about her screw up that she had kept bottled up inside her for the past five days.

When she finished, she had run out of breath and started sputtering. Excusing herself, she sipped the Ginger Ale. Her face flushed to pink. Her heart was racing that felt like a drum beating in her chest.

Rob stared at her in disbelief. His half of the turkey sandwich was untouched. The expression on his face looked as if someone had kicked him in the gonads. Bile rose in Lana's throat and she felt herself getting sick to her stomach. She had waited too long to come clean. Now obvious, if it wasn't before.

"I had the flu," she said in her defense, "and I allowed myself to play that out in front of Vince like I was dying. I didn't know how to tell him. He looks so thin, so pathetic; I wanted to save him from whatever I could save him from, even if it meant being deceitful.

He had slept overnight with Jackie and Megan looking for a new apartment. I wanted him to do that; I couldn't call him to come home."

Lana fell silent, now speechless. She had said too much and yet not enough. Either he was listening, waiting for more, or at some point, he shut down. She understood. She didn't know what else to do or what to say.

Rob couldn't contain his anger. He shouted at her. "Why didn't you call me the first second you discovered the envelope was a bribe?" She flinched. Lana had never seen him so red-faced angry. She took hold of the soda can, and shook it, not realizing it was open. Fizz and bubbles spilled all over. They stared into one another's faces.

"You were on vacation. How was I going to get in touch with you?" She knew she sounded pathetic. He reached for the phone on his desk.

"Are you calling Vince?" she asked.

"Vince? You mean you still haven't told your own husband?" Rob's eyes widened. "Okay, okay," he said. "I'm panicking now. Let's take this slower."

Her legs jiggled automatically. She needed to use the bathroom. She excused herself and ran out of the office and down the hallway towards the ladies' room.

She pushed open the door. Joline was standing in front of a mirror applying lipstick. Lana made a bee-line past her into an empty stall, locking the door behind her. She retched and gagged, shoving her fingers down her throat.

Joline banged on the door. "Lana, what's going on?" Lana remained silent. When she moaned for the second time, Joline banged on the door again. Lana unlocked it and let her in.

"What the hell!" Joline said, pushing Lana's hair away from her face. Standing next to her friend, hoping not to get sprayed by the vile smell coming out of her body.

Joline was gagging. She left Lana in the stall alone. Over the sink, she grabbed a bunch of paper towels and locked the front door of the bathroom so no one else could enter.

Lana sat on the toilet seat with her skirt pulled up as Joline entered and applied cold compresses of paper towels to the back of her neck, moving the little gold cross around her neck to the back of her head. She wiped Lana's face, removed the gook that had gotten into her shining brass mane.

"He didn't take it very well, I gather?" Joline said. "Let me drive you home. You can't stay here looking like this."

"I have to stay" Lana groaned. "I'm going to see Salazar. Larkin had suggested it and now I think he was right. Peter is my friend; he'll always be my friend, and he won't be afraid of helping me."

Joline stood beside Lana, using more paper towels to wipe the mascara blotches from underneath Lana's eyes. "This is the only question I'm going to ask you. Nobody's dead, right?"

Lana shook her head.

"Okay, maybe the flu isn't out of your system yet. Let's get you cleaned up. Put on some makeup. My case is on the counter at the sink."

Lana did as she was told. She washed her face and removed the remaining blotted makeup.

"Please tell Rob I'll be out in five minutes. He's waiting for me." Joline watched as Lana patched-up her face, using blush to add color to her cheeks. She did as her friend had asked her; let Rob know Lana would be back in his office in five minutes. Rob didn't ask Joline any questions. He just nodded his head.

CHAPTER 11

Bureau Chief Peter Salazar rolled down the blinds, shielding his inner-office personnel's view of the internal conversation.

Lana entered his office with her face streaked with blush and tears lingering in her eyes. She looked hungover. Peter Salazar had never seen Lana so frazzled in their seven-year relationship, from her early orientation days as a homicide stenographer on the *Kojack* team.

Lana's reputation preceded het as a quick-fingered, know-it-all, accurate, multi-tasking stenographer. She had been prompted along the way by Vince, who had worked in the homicide division before her. In her own handwriting, she had let the DA's office know beforehand, "Already schooled in autopsy dictation." Salazar had wanted her as his trainee right away.

She now sat across from him, seven years later, with a fistful of tissues in her hand.

"I made a mistake, Peter. And I'm sitting here hating myself."

Salazar had always believed in Lana as tower of strength. He couldn't imagine why she had taken receiving a bribe so hard. She was falling to pieces in front of his eyes.

"Save your strength. You're going to need it," Salazar said. "Your supervisor already let me in on why you were on your way over. The way I see it, you have no reason to hate yourself. You're a human being."

"I'm sick of being so emotional. I can't seem to suck the ears back into my eyes, and I'm completely exhausted."

Lana wasn't apologizing for not reporting the bribe to anyone in authority at the DA's office, or even worse, willy-nilly taking the loaded bribe-money envelope to Chase Bank, handing it over to Larkin. She was feeling bad because she couldn't control her crying.

Salazar looked at her in an odd way, finding her thought-process extremely interesting.

"Take a deep breath," he said, "calm down." He handed her a white handkerchief he from inside the pocket of his dark blue suit.

She waved a fist-full of tissues at him. He took back the hankie, left it on his gray-top desk, and watched Lana as she blotted her eyes.

"I'm not interrogating you," he said. "You're in a friendly environment. Like I said, your supervisor has already alerted me. I agree with Rob. He was shocked you didn't call him, give him a heads up until after you worked in the grand jury, waited until this afternoon to speak to him, kind of adding insult on top.

Her green eyes were water-logged. She stared at Peter, in a plea filled look for him to forgive her. She also wondered how Rob had phrased her fuck-up.

"Listen, Lana, at some point today, you're going to have to give me the details, the facts. Do you have any enemies that might want you to lose your job? Do you have any known family members that are mafia?"

"Strange you ask that. This morning, after five days of ponding those questions in and out of a fever-induced state, those exact thoughts had floated around my head. I don't think I know anyone personally who would want me to lose my job. Not a woman, anyway. Maybe a man who's pissed because I've taken a job away from a man."

"It sounds feasible," Salazar said. "But anything is going to sound feasible at this point. Why don't you go back to last Wednesday and tell me what happened when you came to work that morning," Salazar glanced over at his desk calendar to check dates. "June 16, right?"

"Okay." Lana took a long breath, already exhausted knowing she'd have to repeat the facts of the story, at least the ones she knew, all over again. She guessed she had better get used repeating these things, because Salazar wasn't going to be the last person she'd been telling this story to.

She regrouped, searching her surroundings, the blinds had been closed before she got there; the window behind

Salazar's desk faced the buildings on Court Street; she was able to stare at Montague Street sign on the corner, the exact street where she had run to on that Wednesday morning. She had complete and total recall.

"Wednesday morning, I came to work, got into the office, maybe a quarter to eight. No one was in yet. I had come in early to work on the log for Rob. He had taken a few days off in the middle of the week, using his vacation time. We sometimes have to utilize them, so we don't lose them." Salazar stopped her. Too much fluff.

"Okay, I get that," he said, jotting sentences down on a yellow legal pad.

Lana glanced up at the wall behind his head while he was jotting notes. There were diplomas in frames. One from NYU, Political Science degree, and one from Brooklyn Law School. There were also framed newspaper articles from the *Daily News*, headlines, of cases of murders of the cases he had been part of investigation of David Berkowitz, the serial murder who had killed women based on what he said was messages from his neighbor's dog Sam. That's how the Son of Sam came to be called.

Salazar waved his hand across her face to get back her attention.

"You mentioned keys were missing."

"Yes." She continued to fill tell him more about the keys, not being able to get into her double desk drawer, where she housed her grand jury steno notes.

The phone rang on his desk. "Detective Salazar," he answered. He listened for a minute. "No. Tell one of the other detectives to go out and question him."

He looked towards Lana for her to continue speaking. The window behind Salazar now cracked with a blast of thunder. Further down Montague Street, into Brooklyn Heights promenade Lana saw lightning. She gasped. She searched Salazar's face, who had ignored the weather situation brewing behind him.

"That's standard procedure," she said about her notes. "Grand jury notes were never allowed to just lie around on a desk or be stored in unlocked drawers."

"But you never opened the drawer that morning; is that right?"

"No. Not until today." Salazar's head bolted up. She had never said she had gotten into the drawer earlier in their conversation.

"Okay," he said. "We'll get back to that later."

"The keys weren't there – two small silver keys, the same key, you know, two of the same keys. Not finding them, I dumped the whole correspondence box, all the junk I keep in there. That's when the white envelope fell out."

"Tell me about what the envelope looked like, Outside first, then inside."

"Printed on a business-sized envelope was my name, L-A-N-A L-E-W-I-S. It had my certification initials after my name."

"What does that mean, your certification initials?"

"It's from Albany, State of New York requirement, RPR, stands for Registered Professional Reporter. It certifies passing all tests to work as a stenographer – my license, I guess you'd call it."

"You're saying this envelope had the initials RPR after your name?"

"Yep, just like you said it right now."

"Was the envelope sealed?"

"Yes, it was."

"And when did you open it?"

"Immediately."

"What did you find inside the white envelope?"

"Stacks of hundred-dollar-bills with a folded note written to me."

"Were the bills banded with strips of white paper, like banks usually do with large amounts, you know, denoting specific amounts?"

"No. They were not banded like you'd see in a bank. They were loose, bunched together, squeezed in. That's what it looked like to me."

Peter breathed in deeply.

He felt better now that she appeared calmer. Her eyes were finally dry. She looked intent on wanting him to understand the whole episode, with every nuance that had happened, not leaving out anything. Like she was trying to plant in him what she had experienced, what had happened to her on Wednesday morning.

"Okay," he said. "Why Larkin, why the bank – I mean, it kind of looks fictitious, going to a bank's officer with an envelope full of money, then leaving the money with him to hold onto for you in his safe."

"I panicked after I read the note; you know, feeling threatened, looking around me, surveilling the office, seeing if anyone was hiding. I was scared. I wanted to get out of there immediately."

"Why didn't you come to me?" Her eyes had softened again, looking like two giant peas. Yet, she still appeared overwhelmed, then started to sob. Her sobs were loud like a child who had been punished, uncontrollable sobs, from somewhere deep inside her. Salazar guessed it had nothing to do with the bribe. But what was making her so miserable?

Salazar felt restricted watching her. His first instinct was to rush over to her, hold her in his arms. But they had gotten into trouble once before when he had done that very same thing to make her feel like somebody was listening to her. He wasn't going to add to her problems, or ever put her in that position again. Nor was he going to jeopardize his own career by making such a bold move.

Lana had crumbled in Peter's arms once before on a Friday night after a murder case had come in to be investigated from the 60th Precinct.

When Lana had first come on the scene, she had taken on the reporting job, not only as Peter's stenographer-trainee, but she alongside him as his gal-Friday, pitching in in the file room, which was not her job, but she liked being around him.

Peter had begun to depend on her; on top of her making phone calls and working on transcribing transcripts, she had a knack controlling witnesses that were rambling, slowing them down, getting more coherent testimony, in a nice way, but than any man could have done. She was especially kind to the murdered victim's families.

She had never allowed the intensity of testimony screw up her reporting techniques. If she had to stop a witness, or someone gushing in tears, whatever was taking place during the statement process, she'd put her kindest actions forward. Then in brackets, for the understanding of setting the stage, showing the action of a witness in her final transcripts. She was like a stage director with actors, giving them the floor when necessary and then stifling them was it wasn't necessary for them to speak.

She had used these types of tactics to calm a witness. At times, she looked like the maestro slowing down the beat of an orchestra. She kept whomever the ADA was on a case dignified when they wanted to lash out at a witness, or criminal co-conspirator.

The day she had been assigned to Salazar permanently, he had taken her across to JB's, the usual steak house, all detectives and cops frequented, to celebrate her being added to his division. After two drinks and a steak dinner, he walked her to her car, parked in an out-door parking lot under the Brooklyn Bridge. It was a nice night, the building lights brightened the feeling spring in the air; trees were budding, people were out walking or jogging past them.

"I asked the chief if you could be my permanent stenographer. I hope that's all right with you." Lana blushed. Her green eyes sparkled in the moonlight. She felt flattered. Peter was going places and she wanted to move up the ladder with him. She realized at that moment that she had fallen for him – not exactly in love – but something very real had attracted her to him.

She had been married since she was a kid herself. Seventeen. Of course, she loved Vince and her daughters; but Salazar had excited something inside her that night, when he looked into her eyes and told her he wanted her to be his permanent steno, his permanent riding companion.

He bent over, kissed her on the cheek. She extended her hand to shake like they had firmed up an agreement. Then she felt him pull her in. She hugged him and felt intoxicated by his cologne while his strong body pressed against her. It was just that one time. It had never happened again.

The DA's office had never had a team like these two before, a female steno and a male detective, these two were GQ material, like an Andy Garcia, Meg Ryan kind of couple.

Most of the other detectives enjoyed working with their male counterparts. They could fart, make crude jobs, spit on the sidewalks, tell off-color jokes. A lot of them had claimed they didn't want to get involved with the two new girls on the homicide detail. Salazar had chosen Lana because she had guts, and she also had an English degree while she was a court reporting student. He like that she had understood punctuation and grammar.

She had gotten along well with Peter those first few months. They had rapport from the first day Rob Smith had sent her out with him to cover a homicide that had taken place outside a church in the Greenpoint area of Brooklyn.

Usually, when reporters went riding with detectives, they either bonded or they didn't bond. Lana and Peter were a match. She knew what he expected of her. She had never used the thirty-day contract rule for preparing transcripts of their cases over his head; she had prepared her transcripts almost immediately, or at least within the first week.

Lana wanted the job. She loved the challenge. It had stimulated her. She hoped out of bed in the morning, looking forward to a day of crime and punishment. She knew she had a shot to become a permanent member once she passed the Civil Service test and was placed on the City's list.

Until that test came up, Lana made the best of being a provisional employee, which had turned out in her favor when her husband had gotten cancer. It had been Vince's idea all along to study the stenograph machine. He had been Vince who had become a full-time employee, almost a decade before she had graduated with her certification.

But it had been Anthony's idea, Vince's older brother, who had introduced them to the field of court reporting.

CHAPTER 12

nthony was born two years before Vince. And Vince had always been the baby brother to his older brother's wishes. When the phone call had come about Anthony's life or death situation, Lana couldn't believe her ears. Lana had picked up the phone on the second ring from her bedside table. She had recognized Vince's voice immediately even though he was in a state of panic.

"Lana, honey, my brother Anthony was shot earlier this morning."

Lana gasped, held her breath.

Vince had sounded terrified. "The police are driving me in a police car now, going to Kings County Hospital. I'll call you when I know more."

The phone call had awakened Lana out of a dead sleep. Two small pink baby girls slept in a single crib alongside her. She had a hundred questions going on in her mind, but she had no one to ask. She'd have to wait until she heard back from Vince to learn more about what happened. what part of his body did he get shot, why, and would Anthony be okay.

It had been April 1973. Two weeks earlier, Lana had her hands full when she and Vince had packed up the babies and driven out to Long Island to celebrate Easter Sunday with Vince's parents. Anthony and his wife Debbie had been there, too.

Now Lana wondered if anyone had called her sister-in-law, who had probably gone to work by this time. She looked at the kitchen clock and saw it was ten in the morning. She guessed, if they called Vince, they had probably called Debbie at her job.

She put the phone down. She wouldn't make phone calls. She'd wait it out until Vince called her back. She could pray that everything would be okay, and that Anthony didn't suffer from mortal wounds.

From a teenage boy, Lana had heard stories about Vince's brother, who had always been a rebel rouser. After a long stint of abusing drugs Lana was surprised when Anthony went into the Police Academy. The family had hoped he'd settle down and just do his job and stay out of trouble. Not Anthony. Not his style. Instead, after working six months at a Brooklyn precinct, Anthony applied to be on a narcotics team.

Soon, he worked for the 72nd Precinct as an undercover police officer, a *narc*, short for *narcotics officer*. Anthony worked in two specific areas in Brooklyn to target the buyers and sellers of illegal drugs.

InBay Ridge, not far from where Lana and Vince once lived in a small apartment when they were first married, there was a park that overlooked the Verrazano Bridge, linking Brooklyn to Staten Island. It had become a haven for drug use.

Anthony had also worked another large park in the Brooklyn area. Prospect Park had roller skating and ice skating rinks, where kids could rent horses for an hour. The park was a beautiful playground for kids and their parents to take walks, ride bikes, get out into the fresh air. It had a zoo that housed exotic animals and botanical gardens, ball fields. It added up to over five-hundred acres of activity -- one being where drugs were bought and sold.

Anthony was a convincing narcotics agent. He kept his face unshaven, enjoying the stubble look, and cultivated a Foo Man Chu mustache, pointed downward, touching both sides of his chin. Some days he wore a red bandana, which aligned him with members of a certain street gang. Another one of Anthony's peculiar obsessions was the movies. Days off, he and Vince could be found sitting in any one of ten theaters throughout Brooklyn, but mostly at the Loew's Kings Theatre, sharing a container of milk and a dozen bagels.

Cop movies, action-packed movies, car chases: Vince and Anthony shared a brotherly bond. Anthony, who had once desired to become an actor, had found that being a narcotics agent was the role of a lifetime. Everyone understood why he wanted to play this part. He had been an overweight teenager, and now that he was in peak weight and built, Anthony liked showing off. He inched his way into a black gang, speaking the lingo, practicing characters from movies like *Dog Day Afternoon*. Anthony acted outrageous on the job, hands always moving, like using his fingers spelling out drug names in Indian Sign Language. Only this role ended almost as quickly as it had started.

According to witnesses, as Anthony exited an elevator in a Lenox Hill apartment building, on the fourth floor, Anthony was making a buy, when two piercing shots rang out from a 357 Magnum. The bullets were meant to kill, as the shooter grabbed the buy-money and allowed the elevator door to close, entombing Anthony behind steel doors.

Anthony whore a wire on his chest, recording the activity for a team of police officers who were waiting near the Lenox Hill Apartment House. It was a sting operation.

Anthony tried speaking into the recording, "I'm shot, I'm shot." His team had already moved from their location when they heard the shots.

According to testimony, Anthony lay on the floor of a blood-soaked elevator as the detectives and other undercover police officers stormed the stairwell of the apartment house. Five minutes later emergency vehicles, where more police officers surrounded the complex.

******

Awarded a gold shield, drug dealer captured, Vince Scotto and Anthony Scotto drove together for an entire month to the Criminal Courthouse on Schermerhorn Street, sitting at the prosecutor's table every day of the trial. In that courthouse Vince was introduced to the court stenographer taking the minutes. After few days, Vince cornered the court reporter asking dozens of questions about the job. A new idea, a new career was born for Vince and Lana.

Vince to Lana, "If we work as a team, we could do this."

Vince never saw the truth; he had been star struck by a court stenographer wearing the most expensive suit in the courtroom. He and Lana were kids themselves raising two infant babies; they knew nothing of how the world worked.

PART II

FAMILY SECRETS

CHAPTER 1

It was the late 1950s, and Rita Costanza's fears were lessened by a letter she had received from her cousin Genevieve Rosa. Rita had first written to Genevieve, a month prior, asking for help, for Arturo and Genevieve to sponsor her and her son, to come to the United States.

In the latter she had explained the conditions she and son Luigi had been living under since her husband Vito had been shot gangland-style, leaving she and Luigi to fend for themselves in the cruel world of a Mafia trader.

The letter to Genevieve, captured Italian words: "*Lei e una disgrazia*," (She has been made to feel disgraced for her husband's actions.)

Rita wrote time and time again, "that she had no control over her husband's affairs, and if he had pissed of the Mafia the way he had, why does this penalty fall on me."

The brutal murder of her husband, Vito Costanza, remained unsolved, as Mafia murders usually do. She had heard from other women in the town, that still had talked with her, that the town's *polizia* had never even bothered to investigate Vito's murder. It had seemed, from talk circulating at the port in Palermo, that Vito had betrayed secret Mafia business to a woman friend, and information leaked out to a rival organization, dealing with money-lenders, the type Christ had thrown out of the church in his day, as being the lowest of the low.

Cousin Genevieve Rosa booked Rita passage on the steamship Perugia, scheduled to leave the Port of Sicily bound for the port of New Orleans, Louisiana. Rita brought along her 14-year-old son Luigi. Who soon would be re-christened Costa.

***

Young Luigi may have said many times over several years, after he was safe inside the harbor of the United States, that he recalled every minute of travelling with his mother to America. He remembered feeling butterflies flitting in his stomach and described them to his distant cousins at.

Luigi was fourteen when he had boarded the Perugia from Palermo, Sicily. He and his mother Rita were sponsored by Genevieve and Arturo Rosa. Their passage was paid by these second cousins to Rita, a recent widow.

The boy possessed striking features from the Sicilian side of his family: dark wavy hair and tinted eyes, depending on how the sunlight hit his face. He had inherited his father's good looks on the Costanza side of the family; a man whose good looks got him into trouble with many a woman in his day.

Adding a few words of English into his lexicon, Luigi charmed people mostly with his smile and white teeth. His communications skills were yet to be developed. But he was a nice boy. He possessed manners and charm. Luigi tried communicating the process of entering the country at NOLA – the Port of New Orleans. He had his distant cousins as his audience and started his story with the walk down the gang plank.

"I had stayed close to Mama as we were told to walk outside from the ship to the last wooden thread that held us from being on American soil. But I refused to hold her hand." He rolled his eyes for appeal, as most teenagers might. "I wasn't a toddler. I was a teenager." he said proving his status.

His favorite word was *freedom*, He said freedom in two syllables, putting the accent on both parts. "Free-Dom." He had understood as he crossed the threshold into New Orleans, that this southern population, was a city in the state of Louisianan, where he could walk down the streets without being spit on because he was the son of a mafia trader.

He had conveyed a scary incident to his cousins that had happened on the immigration line. They were all gathered around him, as he admitted he was afraid.

"That's when I grabbed my mother's hand tight as we approached the immigration officer."

The boy had told the story several times to the different sets of cousins who had come to Genevieve's home in the Garden District of New Orleans, to meet the boy, listen to his story about encountering the fearful, official immigration officer, who called the boy and his mother forward on line, to examine their documents.

"The official looked like a mope to me." Luigi said, using the Italian word *sheminudo*," for mope. "He looked like Dopey from The Seven Dwarfs. How could anyone have taken him seriously?"

Luigi made silly faces, showing how the officer had worn his hat tilted on his head, "He looked like a buffoon," the boy roared.

But what had impressed the boy the most about their arrival into the Port of New Orleans was the impressive desk the immigration officer was seated behind. Luigi used his arms, stretching them out five feet as to the length of the desk. He mentioned, "The officer's desk smelled like lemon polish, making the mahogany shine so I could able to see my face in the wood."

Luigi interpreted the once-over the official had given him and his mother by widening his eyes, as the officer, had given the pair a good an efficient look.

"I didn't understand when the officer said for me to take off my hat. He seemed angry." Luigi exclaimed.

"Son," he said, Luigi imitated the officer's voice, giving it have a Southern twang. "Take that damn hat off your head. You're not in New York City."

"At first," Luigi said, "I didn't understand what he meant, 'not in New York City.' But my mother had understood. I was wearing a Yankee's baseball cap. He didn't like that, you know what I mean? That I was bragging to be a Yankee's fan in New Orleans territory."

Luigi admitted to taking the hat off. That's when the officer smiled and started the process of stamping the documents and passport.

"Your child was born in Crete?" the officer asked.

"Yessa," Mama answered. "My husband was in the military at that time when I give birth – have the boy, this son here." She pointed to Luigi.

"The officer stared Mama up and down, you know, like she's was a forger or something. Finally, after a lot of eying us, he stamped our passports, but called me to come back to chat with him." The boy had lost his breath trying to convey how much activity had gone on at their entry point at the port.

"That's when the officer showed me where he had changed my name. I didn't understand what was really happening. Box A, the officer had written in Costa, had taken my last name, turned it into a name that sounded Greek, crossing off the name Luigi. Then in Box B, the officer wrote Lewis, the Americanized version of Luigi.

The officer spoke to Mama about this, even calling her, 'Mama' he said, attempting to being congenial, "Mama, when this kid gets old enough to understand, tell him I have given him a good name. It's going to make it a lot easier for him to live here in America. If you decide to use Luigi, you're going to be – Just use the name the way I have it written here," he said pointing to the document. "*Cap-ee-she?*"

"*Io capissco.*" Mama said, letting the officer know that she had understood what he was talking about. But she really didn't understand and was too embarrassed to admit it.

Later that afternoon, Uncle Arturo translated for Rita her new name, and Luigi's overhaul, into a Greek-Italian immigrant, now living in America.

Costa's final piece of the puzzle came when the officer instructed them to learn how to speak English and learn fast. "Do you understand me?"

Rita answered, "Yessa," with her broken English-Italian accent. "My boy he knows good English. He knows baseball. Tell him."

"Yankees. Play ball!"

From that day forward, Costa Lewis never looked back to his life in Sicily. Those memories were as dead and locked away like his father in his tomb. The change in his name, he had enjoyed for the rest of his time in New Orleans. He never looked back, and he had often mentioned at family gatherings the pride he felt swelling in his chest of being on American soil. He considered it as his second baptism.

CHAPTER 2

Costa continuously sketched out his plan on a sheet of paper now that he was living in the Garden District of New Orleans. At first, he had written, "no mafia attachment, ever" believing, he'd never be recognized as Luigi Costanza, the only son of Vito Costanza, the old-time mafia hoodlum, who had been gunned down in Sicily.

Genevieve and Arturo had believed that they had done God's work, sponsoring the boy and his mother. They enjoyed his presence in their home.

Costa's dark lush hair had reminded Genevieve of the son she had lost in a fatal train accident in Lugano, Italy. Oftentimes, when Genevieve glanced at the photos Rita had sent of her and Costa, Genevieve found it hard to take her eyes off the boy, tracing his fine nose and mouth, experiencing the memories of her son. Costa's expressions and mannerisms, along with his olive complexion, light blue eyes, was so much like her son Paulo.

Genevieve and her husband Arturo, in sponsoring these new potential Americans, were prepared to provide a job at the bakery for the boy. The bakery that was now run by their son-in-law, Mario Sparta, and his partner, Niccolo Giovanni.

Both were dubbed the Cannoli Kings of New Orleans. Arturo was the bakery's founder.

These recipes brought to the U.S by the Giovanni family bakers, boomed in Taormina, Sicily in the 1940s, where they had cultivated an oversized cannoli filled with the family's secret recipe; introducing it to the delight of the American people, using an old-fashioned blending of ricotta cheese, sugar, vanilla, chocolate chips and orange citron, filling the pastry shells on a daily basis, adding the final powdered sugar on top,

Cannoli had become famous throughout the Garden District of New Orleans, served nightly as the after-dinner dolce at the Commander's Palace, a high-end restaurant, located on the same block where Mario Sparta had purchased his new home.

Directly across the street from the Lafayette Cemetery, the basement of the bakeshop resembled a factory, busy daily, trying to keep up with orders, *Numero Uno Pastasterria.*

While Costa worked as the delivery boy at the pastry shop, his mother Rita found work in a brassiere factory. Costa peddled a second-hand bike, delivering Italian bread, while Rita put facets on bra straps, using her thimble fingers to slide the metal objects that allowed women to adjust the height of the bra.

Within a year, sixteen-year-old-Costa, knew everything Mario had wanted him to learn about the world of baking; starting with the customer base, delivering hot steamy Italian loaves, rolls and other baked products, now driven by Costa inside an old beat-up Chevrolet station wagon.

Costa got up an hour later these mornings, rising at seven a.m., making his way to Genevieve and Arturo's, delivering them the first loaves of the day. On one of the mornings when Costa had entered Genevieve's kitchen from the side door, he found himself lingering and drinking the cup of coffee Genevieve had offered.

"Cousin Genevieve, what do you think, my English is much better now?" The charming good-looking teenager had asked. Genevieve praised his ability to have learned to speak English, she pinched one cheek and kissed the other. Pinching cheeks for Genevieve and many older Italian females was a sign of deep affection. That made Costa blush and caused him to say, "Ouch!" in the process.

"You are doing superior, Costa" she said. She thought of saying to the boy, *his English words were like a beautiful strand of pearls, each word a blessing to her ears.*

Instead of being poetic, she was more solemn and preachy.

"Your father can rest in peace now knowing that you and your mother are free from those bad people in Sicily." I tell you," Genevieve said strongly, "*la mafioso* is no good. You are lucky to have gotten out of Sicily alive. Si?" she asked.

"A stupid kid, yes, cousin Genevieve, you are right. But no more." Costa said. Genevieve pelted his cheeks with more kisses. Costa stared at her. Genevieve always appeared to have tears welling up in her eyes. She had soft green eyes, the same as her granddaughter Agnes had inherited. And since Agnes had come to live with Genevieve after her parents were killed in a train accident, she hadn't spoken one word to Costa. She would only speak to Mario's daughter, Maria Sparta.

Agnes had garnered a close attachment to Maria. She shared secrets with her. She was two years younger, like Costa, but not a woman of the world like Maria.

CHAPTER 3

Maria carried both her parents' sur names, Maria Rosa-Sparta; she lived with her parents in the Garden District of New Orleans. Constance Street was a mile away from her grandparents' white mansion. Mario and Theresa's fabulous new home, built to specifications, was located in the middle of a tree-lined block. Living in this is the home Maria considered being one of the worst parts of life. She had come to hate her father. Not her mother as much. She was constantly overwhelmed as the only child and sick of her father's constant preaching.

Mario complained about everything, when it came to his daughter. Her uncombed hair reminded him of a "witch's broom." He said these things aloud to her. On several occasions, to annoy her, he had tugged on his daughter's shirt sleeve, "Why are you wearing, my old flannel shirt?"

Maria tried hard to ignore her father, as best she could, not wanting to get into an argument with him *every* single day. She ripped off his old blue and white checkered flannel to appease him and checked her closet for a girly blouse.

Mario *didn't get* his daughter. Maria *didn't get* her father. Which made the duo agree to disagree?

This new neighborhood where Maria hated growing up, lent its French charm to artists. She wondered why hadn't her father seen this coming? It was the 1960s, and times were a changing.

Constance Street filled blocks with street artists, living in the newly renovated lofts, rooms over grocery stores, pharmacies and bake shops, which made up the demographics of the Garden District. The very reason why tourists came into town. It was the local artists who had attracted the tourist trade on Saturdays and Sundays, the types of visitors who had come specifically to New Orleans to get an idea of how the district had boomed.

Some tourists were artists themselves, even if only in their souls. They appreciated the upbeat music of jazz, the enormous amount of merchandise sold from the sidewalk sales. They had intentionally come to Lafayette Street to explore the creativity of home-made crafts, simple treasures, like wooden jewelry boxes, beaded earrings, silver bracelets, photographic artwork of the cemetery, freshly painted canvasses that they'd hang on their walls when they got home, reminding them later of their visit.

One of the highlights of Constance Street was walking through the world's oldest cemetery. Lafayette Cemetery, dedicated as a historical site of the city, buried their dead in crypts above ground because of flooding problems the area had endured over many years. This was where Maria and her girlfriend Fanny had come to sell their artwork –first by producing it, etching headstones.

They used a fine tracing paper, covered it over the uniqueness of the stones, using a dark but soft led pencil, sometimes colored pencils too, filling in names of the deceased, copying the carved writings and pictures that were on embossed on such tombstones. They sold their art for five dollars a print outside of Lafayette Park.

Mario disapproved of his daughter's passion of tracing tomb stones, he had complained about that oftentimes stained her hands and made her appear unfeminine. He disapproved of her rag-tag style of dress, constantly referring to her as a tomboy. He hated the different color and textured bandana she tied around her forehead, at times, sticking a pigeon's feather in for effect.

He had tried raising her to be a debutante, a feminine product of an Italian household who would go to an Ivy League university. But Maria hadn't taken the lead from the family she was born into. Mario complained even more that Maria wasn't even close to becoming acting like a woman. Like her mother Theresa and grandmother Genieve, whom had cleaned the house, cooked their meals, dressed the part of a wealthy Italian woman; the exact trait handed down from generation to generation.

Maria frustrated her father to the point that he had put mother-in-law on notice that he wanted her, Genevieve, to do extend to him a big favor: "Mama, I have come to you today because I want my daughter to marry Costa, Vito Costanza's son."

Vito Constanza had been deceased for over three years. And because Genevieve had already sponsored Costa along with his mother, Rita, the widowed wife, Mario was pleading with his mother-in-law, that only she could give him hope in his soul for her seventeen-year-old granddaughter.

"I don't understand your rush to marry Maria off," Genevieve said one morning sipping an espresso seated at Mario's new exotic coffee bar at the bakery.

"Mama, my daughter is not likely to attract any boy who lives within the walls of this district, or any other district in our fair city of New Orleans. If you don't do this for me, I'll have to send her away to school, boarding school in Europe, to keep her under control. You see how she dresses every day? Like a pig, a boy, a street bum." Mario was inches away from tears spouting out his words, "She's mean-spirited, and she-- it kills me to say this, Mama, she looks like me." He looked sheepish. His big nose dripping; his face wet with tears.

Genevieve sneered at him. "It's a fad, Mario. All girls go through these phases. They are either too feminine or they like to rough-house it with the boys. You daughter is definitely the latter."

"I love her, Mama, but there have been no suitors. Not one boy at school is interested in her. She's going to be eighteen. Ask Costa. Plead my case. I'll give him a percentage of my bakery. He'll be set for the rest of his life. He owes you, Mama. Talk to him. Please. I can see my wife is losing her mind over our daughter."

"It's different today. It's not like when I got married and was banded together with Arturo by our families. These kids want to do things their own way." Mario looked forlorn as if Genevieve had stabbed him in the heart. In many ways she had.

"I need this curse off my head. Your daughter needs this cup to pass. I fear... You know what I fear most?"

"What? Afraid she wants to be a boy? Now, who's being ridiculous?"

Mario left his mother-in-law sitting at the coffee bar. Talking to himself, feeling defeated and frustrated. His only daughter, Maria. Why was God so cruel? He had seen a vision in his sleep that Maria would bring shame to him and to the family.

That night, Mario prayed to the Lord, down on his knees. When he had awakened the next morning, he had made a pact with himself, and with God, promising to anything, everything he had he'd share with his fellow man.

Going into the front door of the bakery, he had no choice, but to take matters into his own hands.

CHAPTER 4

Aromas wafted into the streets from the ovens of Mario's bakery through the new roof vent, the handy-work of his partner, Niccolo. Since Niccolo had installed the upper vent, hundreds more tourists a month were drawn like to the sounds of the Pied Piper of Hamlin. The sweet fragrances created a dolce-eating frenzy by walkers who came into the bakery after taking a stroll through Lafayette Cemetery. The new coffee bar, also inspired by Niccolo's recent trip to Sicily, had supported more pastry buying and eating; another huge success.

As Mario stepped inside the front door, several customers greeted him.

"Hey, Mario, how's it going?"

"*Bene, bene,*" Mario answered the two men sipping steaming coffee.

But it wasn't *bene bene* at all.

Mario removed the black cap he was fond of wearing and took the dusty white steps to the basement where the ovens smelled like burnt toast. Costa was there, as Mario had counted on, removing the loaves from the oven with a wooden paddle and sliding them onto the white marble countertop.

"Costa, I need you to give me a few minutes, okay?"

"Sure, boss," Costa said, as Mario popped off tops of two bottles of Coke from the cooler and handed one to the boy. They sat on wooden folding chairs away from the heat of the ovens, nearer to the back door that went out to the yard. Costa took a slug of Coke and waited for Mario to speak.

"What do you think of my daughter?" Mario asked the boy. Costa shrugged. This was his boss and Maria had the same big nose as her father. He knew he couldn't say that, so he improvised.

"She's like one of the guys," Costa answered honestly. And that was exactly what Mario was afraid of.

"She doesn't cringe if we curse or spit or scratch our balls. I'm sure that's not what you wanted me to say."

"No, you're wrong. That's exactly what I wanted to hear. I want you to be honest with me. And if you're being honest, then that's what I want to hear. What do you think I can do to get my daughter to become a -- you know, more feminine?

"Your wife, she doesn't know how to do this?"

"Forget my wife. I'm asking you. Tell me. Be honest. I promise I won't be offended," Mario said.

"Barbizon," the boy answered. "Beauty school. Send her to beauty school. Charm school. You see it on television. In magazines. They turn the ugliest woman – sorry! I don't mean Maria's ugly."

Costa suddenly realized he had crossed the line a little too late. Mario waved his hand signaling that it was all right for to speak his mind. Even if it hurt.

"And where does one find these kinds of schools? They are here in the United States?" "Sure. The Yellow Pages. You want me to look for you?"

"No," Mario said. "Now, I must tell you the truth. I want you to cultivate my daughter. I want you to make her feel beautiful. I know you are a year younger than she is, but I want you to marry my daughter."

The Coke Costa gulped too fast, came flying out of his mouth, as the words "marry my daughter," hit his brain. He took the bottle away from his lips and wiped his face on with the bottom of his shirt.

He stared at Mario for a long time. He knew this was his opportunity, his one and only chance to live like his rich cousins had been living all these years while he and his mother suffered through his father's humiliation of fucking up their lives. He knew he had to say the right words. This was not something to screw up, like his father might have. He cautioned himself, *don't say anything, slow down your big mouth.*

"This is between you and me, Costa. I talked to your cousin Genevieve and I had asked her to do me this important favor, to tell you, that I had wanted you to marry my daughter."

Now intrigued that he was being let in on yet another family secret, the boy forced out a grunt.

"I'd never say anything or be disloyal to you. But isn't this kind of old fashioned – not of our generation, to make a marriage like your parents did in the old country?"

Mario appreciated the seventeen-year-old boy was wise to the ways of the world. Mario wondered what they were teaching kids in school, maybe how to be contrary to their parents' thinking.

"I explained to Genevieve that I'd make you a partner in my business if you'd take my daughter's hand in marriage."

Costa hopped off the chair – this was going much too fast now.

"Wait, wait! Don't go. Please hear me out."

The boy sat back down. Marriage was as far away for him as was the war raging in Vietnam. He didn't want to be involved in either one.

Mario stood up. "Listen, son," he said, "I don't mean tomorrow! And certainly not as she appears today. Not in her present state of clothing and attitude. But you'd marry her after her 'coming out' you know, her becoming a debutante."

Costa remained silent. Dumbfounded. Twitching in the chair. He tried to picture Maria with a new nose. They do those things now. Women can have nose jobs, boob jobs, all sorts of jobs. Costa's expressions remained sullen, not distressed as when he first heard the offer. Mario was still talking, and he wasn't paying attention. He snapped himself back to listening to who might be his future father-in-law.

"Listen, boy, you owe me your confidence. Don't say anything to anyone. Do you promise?"

Costa raised his hand like being sworn in as a witness in a court of law. "I promise," he said. "I have always appreciated you as a good and caring father, Mario. Maria is just feeling her oats. In time, she'll come around."

Tears welled in Mario's eyes. Maria was the only daughter he was ever going to have, and he wasn't going to let her ruin her life and regret it forty-five years later.

CHAPTER 5

osta did his part in wooing Maria and Mario, putt his money where his mouth was. Mario paid for special art classes, the kind Maria had always wanted. He allowed her to take ballet, even though he believed she looked like a clumsy oaf.

Four months after Costa had started dating Maria, without anyone knowing, other than he and Mario, Maria asked her father if she could have a nose job. Mario had gone this far. What was a couple of more thousand dollars to fix her broad chin at the same time?

"Go pick her up," Mario said to Costa. "She'll be glad to see you waiting for her in the car." Mario handed Costa the keys to his black Cadillac Seville. "She's got a big ass, so be careful when you're parking her." The boy removed his bakery apron and chuckled heartily.

"I wasn't sure for a minute who you were saying had a big ass."

Mario finally cracked a smile in the face that had turned into stone from aggravation over the years that his daughter had given him grief. Mario now believed that things were finally working out. He owed Costa big time. And he'd never stiff the boy on the deal that he had made--offering him a percentage in the bakery business.

Every week, Mario handed Costa a small white bank envelope with one per cent bonus on the revenue. Things were going pretty good now at store Number Two.

He had gotten his daughter in check. He and his wife had settled down and stopped throwing fits over their Maria. Things were peaceful in their household, finally.

Mario sat and watched television in the evenings, feeling like a regular human being, laughing at some of Ed Sullivan's gestures, especially when he announced, "Folks, tonight is going to be a really good shoe." Costa and Maria were either on the front porch, taking a walk or going down to the soda fountain for ice cream.

Mario's head was back to more important things, like business opportunities on the rise, new places for him and Niccolo to branch out. They had recently talked about opening a franchise in Little Italy in New York City. If Costa kept his promise to never to tell Maria that her father instituted the idea of their dating, ultimately planning on marrying Maria off, Mario might see his way clear to allow Costa and Maria, after they were married, of course, to travel to New York City, to scope out a new business.

Costa's brain wasn't dead, like so many kids that functioned wildly. Mario experienced a shift, the burden of worry now lifted from his shoulders. Maria's antics and lifestyle had weighed on him like a boulder. And now, she was sweet, offering him kisses on his check.

"Thank you, Poppa, for allowing me to take art classes. I love them so much. I don't even mind getting up early in the morning. The other girls and boys are like me – they are introspective and creative, and I find myself thinking that one day I'll be a great artist."

Mario blushed from his neck to the top of his head. Maria had never thanked him for anything before. She had seemed self-centered and out of control – her behavior towards her mother had softened too. They were talking about clothing, where she should shop, what shoes went with dresses and slacks.

Being loved by someone made all the difference in the world in his daughter's personality. He almost couldn't believe the change in her.

And Costa had stayed true to the deal he and Mario had made. He never told anyone about the conversation in the basement that he had had with Mario, about taking Maria as his fiancée.

Years later, whenever he thought about what Mario had proposed to him, he smacked himself on the forehead and cried saying, "What a young fool I was talked into that mess."

CHAPTER 6

As the mess of saying yes to marrying Maria had continued to engulf Costa, sucked him into the Sparta family and the riches they possessed, the beat goes on, taking Costa two months, moving forward, to the engagement day. Suddenly Costa can't take it anymore. He is bursting to tell someone.

Costa goes to Genieve's to find out exactly what Mario had said to her initially.

Agnes walked out from her bedroom, wondering who had come into the house.

Upon seeing her, Costa was fidgeting with keys in his hand, asks her; "Agnes, do you know where your grandmother is?"

"Not really," she said. "It's Tuesday. Maybe she's at the bakery." Costa paced the kitchen like a man going to the electric chair. Upset due to his own stupidity and greed, he knew better than to confide in Agnes as to why he was looking for her grandmother.

Instinctively, he believed females were in cahoots. If he were daring enough to say anything about the engagement or marrying Maria, especially now that the date had been pushed up significantly, it could come back to bite him on the ass.

"Can I—assist you, cousin?" Agnes stumbled on the appropriate word to make herself clearer in English.

Costa offered her an English translation. "Help," he said. "In Italian – the verb *aiutaire*. Let me hear you say *aiuto* in English. Go ahead, you say the word help.,"

"Help, yes. Si, *aiuto* is I help."

"Good. If you practice a different English word every day, you will learn even faster. Of course, you must tell people to speak slower. These crazy Americans. The people here speak like crazy people in this county."

"Genevieve, I think, Genevieve, she goes to French Quarter to buy lace."

"*Bene*," Costa says in Italian, meaning that she had phrased her sentence correctly.

"I show you how I know to speak English. Tuesday, Thursday, Wednesday," Agnes said, then started laughing. She had tricked Costa into believing that she didn't know how to speak English. What Costa hadn't known was that her father was a professor in Lugano. And she and her father had spoken oftentimes times in English when he was alive.

"You were making a fool of me. The way you said those days of the week, that's a line from the *Godfather* movie." Her eyes lit up on fire, bright and alive, as Costa joked with her. Her long blonde curly hair fell over her shoulders. Her pale green eyes, the same as Genevieve's and like Maria's sparkled like a cat's.

Agnes sat in a chair at the kitchen table, smacked the top of the seat next to her, and Costa sat down.

"You in trouble?" she asked him.

"Not so much in trouble, you know, like bad trouble. Maybe it's good trouble. I wanted to see Genevieve, because she's a scoundrel, and she had known all along what Mario had in mind for me at the bakery."

"It's a secret?" she asks him.

"For now, it's a secret. But later, it won't be. Don't ask me anything else. Please."

"Okay," she said, happy with herself for having Costa's attention.

"You go to work now?"

"No. I'm finished for today. What do you do all day in this house by yourself?" he asked.

"Come," she said, "I'll show you."

The bright hallway weaved around a close door that went down to the basement where Arturo had built a cardroom and a bar for the adults to hang out. There was a juke box with forty-fives from the fifties and sixties. Costa enjoyed being allowed to press the buttons on some of his favorite Elvis tunes.

Beyond the basement door, inside a lavender and white-painted room, an extra bedroom had been created. The room had a dresser loaded on top of it with tubes of paint – against the walls, canvasses, some finished, others blank, Costa guessed this was where Agnes spent her days occupying her time.

No one had ever spoken about Agnes' artistic work. Costa had no idea she was a talented artist, which was probably why Maria wanted to learn new and different painting techniques. Agnes' favorites appeared to be painting white lilies held up high on tall green thick stems. There were several pictures in the room, one that looked like a villa in a densely populated jungle, ivy wrapped around trees and a monkey sitting on one of the top branches. Costa was impressed.

The room had full sunlight. A soft breeze parted the sheer curtains, opening them up enough to see out onto the large brick patio in the backyard.

Agnes sat down on the bed, which was covered with shades of green and rose sorbet bedding with pillow shams to match. A typical girl's room, Costa thought, which totally fit Agnes' femininity.

She patted the bed, the same way as she had tapped the chair, for him to sit next to her. He did as he was told like someone in a hypnotic state. He instantly felt awkward. Standing up, he realized he shouldn't have acted so casually. But like Maria, Agnes was his second – or maybe third cousin, well, second cousin once removed. Although she looked like a mature woman, he knew she was only sixteen, at best.

He couldn't help noticing her full breasts, so unlike Maria's flat chest. He also noticed she wasn't wearing a bra. He felt his pants rising with every second he kept looking at her breasts. If he made a move to get up and go, he was afraid she might see his excitement.

"Please sit next to me, Costa," she said, "I promise to behave."

"Your English is good," he said. "Were you scamming me?"

"Scamming?" she asked.

"You know exactly what I mean, don't you?"

She laughed. He pretended to smack her, and she grabbed his hand and put it on her breast.

"I want you," she said. "I've wanted you from the first day I laid eyes on you."

He quickly removed his hand from her soft hard breast, almost like he had touched fire. Only he had liked what he felt, the hardness of her nipples. He had never touched Maria in this way. They had kissed, of course, getting to know one another. But nothing quite like this.

"What do you mean? I am promised to your cousin."

"You know what I am saying, Costa. I want you to fuck me."

Costa jumped up off the bed. He had no heard girls speak like this before. Then he remembered Maria's potty mouth.

"Costa, just once. One time before you marry that pig of my cousin." His eyes widened

She had already known. Maria must have told her. "I can't do that. Are you crazy?"

"Yes, maybe I am a bit crazy. It's wonderful to be crazy and spontaneous like this. I know what I want, and I want you. I've done this before at school. I know how to make boys crazy."

As a virgin himself, Costa couldn't believe his ears. "What if Genevieve –" Agnes pulled him on top of her.

"She's not coming home. She is with Arturo. They are out for the night shopping, then the theater."

Agnes removed her scant tee-shirt. Costa couldn't believe his eyes. His dirty magazines weren't as luscious as Agnes' breasts in full color.

"Get under the covers and take off your pants," she demanded. Costa did as he was told and prayed he would not ejaculate when she touched him.

She smelled like roses and lavender, honey and vanilla. How was that even possible to smell like a botanical garden, he wondered?

Agnes removed her shorts. She wasn't wearing any underwear, either. What kind of a girl was this? He didn't care. He didn't care at that moment. He wanted to feel her skin, smell her hair, sink into her body. And she wanted that too. She allowed him to touch her where he had never touched a female before. And when it was over, they both had breathed so hard they had become hysterical with laughter. When the phone jingled on her dressing table, Costa panicked, grabbed for his pants and shirt, leaving his underwear underneath the covers of her bed. He had also left his semen inside of her.

CHAPTER 7

Genevieve had purchased exquisite white lace in the French Quarter for Maria's bridal veil. The seamstress had cautioned Maria not to put on any weight. "No eating hamburgers and French fries." Photographers were scheduled to take engagement pictures of the happy couple for the *New Orleans Times*. "You don't want to embarrass yourself," the haggard old biddy with the wart on her chin exclaimed.

When Costa arrived at Genevieve's kitchen door most mornings, he peeked in first, not wanting to see Agnes, because he knew he'd never be able to keep his eyes off her. Agnes had never called him once since that day in her bed; she had never gone to the bakery to see him, catch a glimpse of working. It was as if their encounter had been a figment of his imagination.

"Once," she had said. "Once." She had only wanted to fuck with him once?

Is that right? He couldn't stop thinking about her, even while kissing Maria. He remembered the feel of her skin, even while Maria edged closer, putting her hand inside his thigh. *Amazing how these Italian girls were all hot to trot!*

No different in Sicily. The young girls had been more curious than the boys. Boys wanted to play ball, drive in cars. So many times, he had heard stories of teenage girls performing sexual acts on boys, but never allowing a boy to penetrate them.

What if Agnes had gotten pregnant? The fear coursed through his body. *What if that was her plan?* To get pregnant by him and screw up his life, his plans of becoming rich. *No! Can't happen. She wasn't that kind of a girl.* But he wasn't a mind reader, how could he even begin to know what she was or what she wasn't?

He felt incapacitated to move from the basement chair, where he was supposed to be filling cannoli for the evening's supply for several local restaurants. Sweat dripped from his forehead and into the sweet mixture in a vat in front of him. He took a spoon and removed a portion of the ricotta cream and put it in his mouth. It tasted and smelled like citron, like Agnes. Sweet and delicious. She had been a dessert, one he had never tasted before. How would he get her out of his taste buds?

He planned on seeing her one more time. He had to. He felt like a man possessed, like a drug addict, something he had witnessed watching an old Italian movie, *The Rose Tattoo*. The actress and actor were in lust. He understood what that meant now, because he was going crazy with the scent of Agnes inside his nose and the taste of her on his tongue.

"Oh, *Deo*, help me. Please."

PART III

TEMPTATION HAPPENS TO THE BEST HUMANS

CHAPTER 1

Monday evening, after many hours, explaining her actions to both her supervisor and to the Bureau Chief of the Organized Crime Unit, Lana returned home. Vince did not come out to greet her. Lana figured he had heard the car hitting the bump in the driveway, as she always had the same problem, backing into the garage. She had also hit a heavy rubber garbage bin, knocking the contents over, and Vince still did not come out front to see if she was all right.

Lana picked up the smelly garbage and dragged the container down to street level for removal the next morning. At the front door, she inserted her key and opened the door. Still no Vince. Pictures of her daughters hung on the blonde paneled wall from every phase of their lives: depicting the era of braces, zits, until they blossomed in lovely pretty women.

The house felt cooler than the outside air, and she was relieved to be indoors. Her stomach ached from retching. Her eyes still puffy and red. She thirsted for a cold beer and to lie down in the den, and just zoon out.

Stepping into the kitchen, she spotted Vince through the glass patio doors. He was sitting at the picnic table facing the kitchen. He had a stack of pages in front of him, the obvious proofing of a transcript. A pencil sat on the table next to him. There was also a slim bottle of Corona to his left.

Lana's mouth watered. She dropped her bags on the terracotta floor, finally causing Vince to turn his head and see her standing inside the kitchen. Her heart dropped when he didn't come in to greet her. She tried holding back her emotions and glanced out towards the garden, hoping her emotions wouldn't spill over again.

Out back, the flower garden was one of Lana's favorite places. As she peered out the kitchen window, beneath the weeping willow tree there were two birdhouses, one that belonged to Jackie and one was Megan's. She and her daughters had planted the willow when they had moved into the house. Now in full bloom, the willow spread its branches in the shape of an umbrella. Each slender green blade mirrored fine silk ribbons, dramatically bowing in her presence. As leaves dropped, they spiraled like tops onto the ground.

Lana drew in a breath taking in her surroundings. It didn't help get her emotions in check. The usual chirpy birds tweeted in the branches as if nothing could possibly be wrong in the world.

Lana hated the new and seemingly ever-present imbalance of her emotional threshold. She hated herself more for having made a horrible mistake, being impulsive, coaxing her husband's friend Jay to corroborate, never thinking once to place a phone call to Vince's for his guidance. And now, it seemed clear that Vince had heard about it all and was terribly wounded.

What makes me tick? Maybe never really having a man in her early life, meeting Vince on a bus stop when she was sixteen. He had been engaged once before, to an older woman When they'd first met at the bus stop, it seemed he saw her as child-like baby doll, a Sandra Dee. He had fallen in love with her and made no bones telling his parents and brother that she was the cutest check ever.

During their courtship, she clung to the handsome court reporter, who was working his way through school, and ringing up groceries in the A&P. It seemed to Lana that Vince enjoyed "parenting" the fatherless young woman. It was probably not something he intended to do, but it had just happened. She looked up to him. Well, he was over six feet tall with a slender build. And she wanted a man's opinion. Yet, she felt vulnerable under a man's control. There was this indestructible personality inside Lana, a superhero trying to get out of her body and become her own person.

How had she and Vince gotten to this place nontalking aspect of their marriage? Had he been jealous of her working with Detective Salazar? She had never crossed the line with Peter – what did cheating mean anyway. Sex? She had never had an affair with Peter – but she had enjoyed his company and working with him. As Joline had mentioned, "He certainly is eye candy." Peter was that -- always tan and lovely, strong and handsome. Because Lana thought that way about him, was that cheating on Vince? Enjoying her job, being in Peter's company, even loving her job, and depending on Peter occasionally?

She sensed that the fact Detective Salazar wasn't married bothered Vince. And possibly working the nighttime shift with a young good-looking available bachelor.

Peter never had crossed that line with a woman. He could have been fired if he had. Whatever Lana and Peter had accomplished in their every-day working situation, had been above board. That is, until the night a call came in about an alleged homicide in the Graves End section of Brooklyn.

Graves End, a section of Brooklyn is located an exit before Coney Island off the Belt Parkway sounds awfully spooky. But in reality it had always been known as quiet neighborhood with homes and apartments-- many rented out as professional sites.

During the statement-giving process, Lana, fingers flew across the keys of the machine, while Detective Salazar, wearing a dark-colored suit, his raven hair slicked backed that touched the collar of his white shirt, conversed privately with the prosecutor. ADA David Marlonallowed the witness to make a phone call to his wife, who had no idea he had found a dead body in the alley of his mother's East 2nd Street home.

The interrogation of the witness had ended when the prosecutor said, "No further questions for this witness at this time."

Lana marked the time ended on her paper, as 9:23 pm. She packed up her equipment. Peter asked Lana if she was hungry.

She nodded in the affirmative, agreeing to go to JB's, a popular steakhouse in the neighborhood.

Upon entering the restaurant, a few locals were still seated at tables eating dinner. Lana and Peter sat themselves at the bar.

"Two vodka martinis, olives," Peter announced to the bartender, a hairy fellow, with a long white beard and braided white hair took their order and prepared their drinks.

They clinked glasses, avoiding spilling a drop, Lana sipped, Peter stabbed an olive with toothpick, and they began chewing the fat about work. As natural a conversation for them as two cooks sharing recipes.

Lana had lost track of time, showing off her newly acquired detective skills. One of those John Jay course books she had picked up that delved into the criminal mindset.

"You really do believe you have an Angela Lansbury trait?" Peter asked. Lana threw her head back and laughed. Her eyes were bright and shining as she munched at her martini-drenched olives waiting for a hamburger and fries to arrive.

They mutually discussed the homicide they had just taken testimony of. The witness, who was leaving his mother's house, locked her front door, heard shots ring out from approximately two or three doors up the street.

Because it had snowed earlier in the day, the witness, during his testimony, said he had a hard time maneuvering down the icy steps of his mother's rowhouse. It had taken him five or six minutes – then he had decided to turn back, because he thought he should mind his own business, not put himself at risk – but something told him, his word, to walk back towards the sound of the gunshots.

After he found a body lying in the alleyway, he called the police and did not go further to see if the man was alive. He made it very clear that he did not approached the body. But he yelled out, "I'm calling the police, hang on, Mister."

*****

According to the morning headlines in the *Daily News*, several mechanics were called to come down to the police station to give their testimony. That part of the investigation had been handled by the next shift of detectives and a morning shift stenographer.

Reading the newspaper, the following morning, Vince pointed to Lana to the headlines.

"I see you were the stenographer on this case," Vince said while eating breakfast at the kitchen table.

"I know you're not psychic," she said. "Where are you getting your information from that I was the stenographer?"

Vince, in a deliberate manner, licked his index finger, turned each page until he reached to page 6 of the *Daily News*, where a photo of Lana appeared, pulling up her notes for a read-back of the statement she had reported.

Two sentences beneath the picture announced: "Lana Lewis, one of the first women machine stenographers at the

Kings County DA's office, takes a statement of a testimony to a crime committed in the driveway, a few doors away from his mother's home. He immediately called the homicide division at nine-twenty on the night of February 5, 2000."

Lana had never come home after her shift had ended on February 5, 2000; she had decided to have another drink with her partner in crime, Detective Peter Salazar.

Vince wondered had his Barbie-Doll wife, who married him at seventeen years old, and he was an old man of twenty-four, had she grown weary of him, staying out on a murder cases than at home with the old man.

*****

Lana had no trouble recalling when she and Vince were passionate lovers, holding on to each another well into the early morning hours; their bodies and their breath as one.

After becoming a member of the homicide team in the early '80s, Vince worked into the night preparing transcripts. The part of the job no one ever tells you about. The evening cuddle fests cooled down. There were more important jobs as stenographers and parents, their two young daughters starting their first semester in Binghamton University. Making money became the number one goal in the Scotto household. As a court reporter, the mainline to making the *do-re-me* meant, *hi ho, hi ho, it's off to work we go*. If that isn't your main reason for becoming one of these extremely skilled professionals, then you've entered the wrong job. The flood gates are open – the daily copy rates for transcription are through the roof. It's dollar signs, dollar signs, dollar signs. There isn't a court reporter alive working the job that isn't making hand over fist.

Lana broke the strange silence, "Vince, can we please talk?"

He lifted his eyes from the page he was reading, laid down the hundreds of words, going from left to right and the page, and placed it down on the picnic table.

"You have no idea how sorry I am that I didn't call you about..." Lana didn't even know what to call it anymore, "the bribe," "the attempted bribe" "the envelope"? She kept her mouth shut, allowing him the opportunity to speak.

"Gee, Lana, that was over a week ago," he said, his voice heavy with sarcasm. It was usual for Vince to throw things back at her, jumping on the defensive immediately.

"Not quite a week," Lana said, trying to minimize the damage, hopping on defense herself. "Please just listen," she begged him. He nodded his head and didn't say another word.

"When I got into the office last Wednesday, at first I didn't notice the envelope right away. I was preoccupied trying to find my keys to unlock my drawer."

"Okay," Vince said. "Look at you now, Lana, you're up to your eyebrows in bureau chiefs and detectives."

"Vince, please, I didn't do anything wrong. The envelope was sitting in that box long before I got there that morning. I didn't provoke this bribe, or whatever you want to call it. I didn't talk to anyone. I didn't meet – I didn't do anything. Can you please keep that in your mind that I'm the god-damned messenger here?"

Vince gave in and nodded his head.

CHAPTER 2

gnes dragged a lawn chair and placed it against the brick wall of the bakery. She closed her eyes and listened to the sound of never-ending traffic moving over her head on the Brooklyn-Queens Expressway. She pictured her estranged niece, Lana, and wondered whether she had found the envelope she had left for her that morning.

Agnes wore a sardonic grin on her face, hoping she had managed to scare the wits out of the girl. If her bitch of a mother, Maria, were still alive, Costa might have twisted Agnes's arm to give the stack of hundred-dollar bills to her. Agnes, determined, in her thinking, could have accepted that challenge.

Maybe giving thousands of dollars away to his daughter might be looked at as a nice gesture on Costa's part, wanting to come out as the good guy, letting Agnes go down in the Rosa books as being the criminal. Sure, her grandfather Arturo had given Costa money for Marie-Elaina, but that was thirty years ago. She guessed he was trying to get his soul ready for heavenly place. But what about my kid? What about Junior?

Agnes had hoped that leaving a bribe on the court reporter's desk, asking her to lose her notes, might in some way ruin the girl's reputation when word got out, in the hope of damaging her credibility as a court reporter.

Agnes drew on a memory in her head, picturing Lana wearing an expensive red woolen cape. In the secrecy of her thoughts, she had referred to the girl as a "whore." She thinks she's important. Wait until I finish with her, then everyone will know her name.

Agnes made the sign of the cross across, touching her forehead, her chest, and then putting her finger on her right shoulder and then her left.

"Thank you, Almighty God for divine intervention. It had to be you who provoked one of our customers to leave the newspaper open to the page where Little Miss Redhead, wearing her red winter cape, so cute and so sophisticated became the community story on Page 5."

"Twooo," she spit, on Lana's picture. "First woman. First woman. First woman. You'd think she was the goddamned First Lady. I'll never let you forget I was the first woman your father got pregnant. Do you hear me?"

Agnes looked around at her surroundings, realizing she was blaspheming the girl out loud. She shut her eyes to pretend she was asleep in case Junior looked in her direction. But he never looked at her anymore with any kind of love in his heart. From two slits of her eyes she squinted to see her son; Junior, had his half his arm inside the refrigerated box, scooping a cup of cherry ices for another customer.

Niccolo felt his mother's eyes on him. He glared back at her and wondered what she was thinking. She was such a pathetic soul. He felt sorry for her. She had suffered many hardships as a young girl, the main one becoming pregnant with him.

The Rosa family ex-communicated her as a slut who might ruin the entire female household. They sent her to a convent in the French Quarter, a long way from the white mansion on Constance Street. Agnes moved all her things into the convent, where she spent the rest of her pregnancy cooking and cleaning, where no one knew where she was, except Niccolo Giovanni, the man who had become Junior's legitimate stepfather.

Junior broke her thought pattern.

"Mama, do you want cold water or maybe a cup of lemon ices?" "No, I am fine," she said. "But move me. The sun is bothering my eyes."

Niccolo stepped outside from his booth behind the window. Agnes stood up and Niccolo moved her chair. She had gotten shorter over the past couple of years. She was also wrinkled. No longer the beauty he had heard she once was; the woman who had given birth to him in a nun's bedroom, where a crucifix hung on the wall. A simple room, he remembered learning how to run in. The place where he had coloring books and toys that Niccolo Giovanni had brought to him on Sundays when he visited.

Junior remembered her vibrant and happy, even though they were alone, without a real father and grandparents. The elite bakery giants.

Junior was embarrassed that he couldn't look at his mother's boney frame. She had stopped doing her hair. She had ditched the ritual of going to the beauty parlor when they had first moved to Brooklyn, along with all her clean and fashionable dress. She never changed out of dirty housedresses, going to feed pigeons looking more like a bag lady than Niccolo Giovanni's rich wife.

Niccolo Junior had once read a book that a priest had loaned him when he'd go to confession. *Hind's Feet on High Places*. Junior enjoyed reading the book; understood its message. For some reason, reading its words, always reminded him his mother, her pain and suffering through the years.

Before Junior's birth, while still pregnant, the family found out Agnes had been with child. The cousin she now hated, Maria, had spread the word of this blemish that had stained the young Agnes. Agnes had never confessed to whom the child's father was. The family didn't quite throw stones like in biblical days, but that would have been less painful. They had encouraged Agnes to live at the mother house on Fairmont Street, a section of the French Quarter where pregnant girls were taken in by the Sisters of Charity.

While at the convent, Agnes dwelled on Maria, whose arranged marriage was set to take place on her eighteenth birthday; she was the one who had turned the entire family against Agnes behind her back. At a family gathering, in the Rosa's backyard, Maria had chosen to mock Agnes for gaining weight, bringing attention to the girl's rounded stomach.

The more Niccolo read from the *Hind's Feet* allegory, the more he had begun to understand: There will always be people who had to deal with pain and suffering all their lives, and are hopefully transformed, will come to know and receive Grace and Glory as their constant companions.

As far as Niccolo could tell, his mother had not been raised up to the glorious state. As for grace, she had lost any grace she might have possessed as a very young girl.

Niccolo Junior had to concede, his mother had given up her life for him. He had yet to know how to be loyal to her and pay her back for the anguish she had experienced.

CHAPTER 3

*I*f only it were true: that time heals all wounds.

A settlement is an agreement that takes place between two or more parties; the party of the first part, and the party of the second part, for less than each one wanted to settle for. It's those types of agreements where no one is happy. Only the judges participating in getting the people to agree on such an idea.

It's courtroom language, sign on the dotted line, and no one walks away from the table happy.

Lana had always believed those scenarios, in the legal terminology of words used, even about her own marriage, she had reconciled with this idea years ago: she and Vince were stubborn to the core. Maybe they would never come to an agreement, a stipulation, or a settlement.

*****

Inside the building situation at 190 Joralemon Street, Kings County District Attorney's office, sat Detective Jack Poggibonsi, a rugged looking old-time cop, who wore a thick black mustache plastered under his nose. Alongside him was his sidekick Shawn Schneider, a redheaded cop, only on the job only a few years. Shawn made it to the heights of detective status, working alongside his mentor Poggi, as everyone called him, when arresting Angela Davis one night at a party upstate New York, where a gun was found in her purse that had been involved in recent murders in Brooklyn.

Shawn had just gotten the assignment via telephone from Bureau Chief Salazar's office to meet up with Poggibonsi, and talk to, not interrogate a Niccolo Giovanni, Junior at the Van Brunt section of Brooklyn at an Italian Bakery named Numero Tre.

This Number Three bakery is the companion bakery of the Number Uno and Number Dos, the owners being one in the same, Mario Spata from New Orleans and Niccolo Giovanni, also from New Orleans, Agnes and Niccolo Giovanni – previously opened two decades ago by Maria and Costa Lewis.

As the detectives thumbed through this information, secured from the Clerk's office of Kings County, before getting out to the car, they started to piece together the previous owners and the latest owners of this bakery enterprise.

*****

Poggi exited the black undercover Taurus, stepped inside the bakery, and asked to speak to Niccolo Giovanni, Junior. Niccolo Junior, a short balding man, dressed bakers' whites, came out from behind the counter, agreeing to speak with the detectives.

The men sat around a circular ice cream parlor table, looking like they had swallowed the red pills in an Alice in Wonderland scene.

Poggi started his questioning first. "Do you know a woman by the name of Lana Lewis?" Niccolo Junior's expression was stiff, his overweight body rigid.

Poggi interpreted Junior's attitude as a man who had almost peed his pants when he heard the name Lana Lewis.

"No," Niccolo Junior lied. "That name doesn't sound familiar to me, Detective. Why? Did she say she knew me?" Poggibonsi gave Junior a twisted look, meaning, are you kidding me, kid, I don't see any women lining up around the block for you.

Niccolo Junior asked, "Detective, should I have a lawyer present?"

"That's up to you. You're not under arrest -- I mean, except for the bookmaking charge that you'll be facing with your father. Think of this as an every-day questionnaire, like I'm writing a story about you."

"If you tell me I'm not being arrested, or accused of anything, then I don't need my lawyer. I believe you."

Poggibonsi turned to his partner, and asked him to step outside for a few minutes. Schneider looked pissed off, getting dismissed in front of a dickhead, but he got up from the chair and walked out of the bakery, lit up a cigarette, leaning his body against the black Ford Taurus. Inside the shop Poggi had started questioning Junior.

"Niccolo, I'm going to come clean with you, son. Because I know you have enough shit going on your plate. This woman, Marie-Elaina, maybe that's the name you know her by, or her nickname Lana, she's a court reporter, you know, one of those gals who sits in a courtroom with a machine tucked in between her legs." Poggibonsi laughed when he realized what he had said. Niccolo Junior smirked too.

"She doesn't sound familiar, detective" Junior replied. Poggibonsi shifted his body, leaning the tiny swirled-back chair, pushing his face, pushing on his thick black mustache with his thumb and index finger, closer to Junior's face. He whispered in his ear.

"She's a grand jury reporter. A redhead you can't miss, you know, a hot chick, who always wears short skirts, nice legs." Niccolo's face froze over.

"Grand jury. What's that got to do with me?"

"Good question, kid." The detective shook his head, deciding to tell Niccolo Junior about the attempted bribe. "I'm going to let you in on a little secret, but that's gonna stay right here between the two of us. Capisci?"

Junior looked at the detective as if to say, since when did you and I become goombahs? Poggibonsi removed the small black comb from his back pocket and ran it through his mustache. Junior watched but didn't dare crack a smile.

"Someone left this reporter a stack of hundred-dollar bills and asked her to lose grand jury notes on your father's case. You understand what I'm saying,' lose grand jury notes' maybe burn them, get rid of them. I bet you can guess what I mean."

"Detective, I have no idea where you're going with this." Niccolo, doesn't appear to be the sharpest knife in the drawer, is totally clueless what any of this has to do with him.

"Your indictment, your father's indictment. She was offered a bribe by someone on your behalf, his behalf, a lot of money, to take those notes and throw them away. That's a felony, kid. Maybe the reason for the bribe was to stall until you get an eye witness to help you out, or somebody gets whacked. Understand? That was all on your behalf, Niccolo, for your case not to go forward, better yet, delayed, postponed, something like that. But even if we say you know what I mean?"

"Detective, I didn't write no note, I didn't leave no money. Believe me. It wasn't me. It's not a murder indictment. I was holding paper, numbers, illegal gambling. I thought you were coming here today to arrest me. I'm serious, detective, when you called, that's what I thought. I swear I haven't done nothing wrong."

Poggibonsi uses a tough-stare, glares at Niccolo Junior as beads of sweat were forming across his forehead. Niccolo was feeling something more than the heat coming out of those big ovens in the basement – Poggi thought litmus test. I'm going to put his feet to the fire.

"Okay, son," Poggibonsi said and slapped Niccolo on the shoulder. "Yeah, kid, you're right; you're clean. I mean it, I believe you. But someone attempted to bribe a court reporter on your behalf and on your father's behalf. It's a felony to bribe a public servant." Niccolo's whole body slumped like someone let the air out of a balloon.

"Listen to me, kid, I want you to give this a lot of thought." The detective handed Niccolo Junior his card. "Call me if you remember something, or if you find something out."

Junior's white shirt had armpits stains, wet rings of sweat on his nice white bakery shirt. His face went stiff holding onto the detective's card.

"Remember what I said, this was a private conversation. The only other person who knows I'm here is Detective Schneider, who's out there smoking his lungs out." Poggi pointed to Schneider leaning against the Black Taurus.

Junior lifted his eyes to peek through the doorway. The detective looked all spit and polished like an SS Officer, blowing smoke rings out of his mouth.

"No, sir, I swear. I won't talk to no one about this. I can't think of anyone who would do anything like for me or my father."

Schneider was pissed off when Poggibonsi walked out the front door towards the undercover police car.

Poggi got in on the driver's side and started up the Taurus. As they pulled away from the Van Brunt Numero Tre, Poggi said to Schneider, "Let's go talk to the court reporter again."

"No can do, Jack. Chief Salazar will pull you off the case. He's got this girl under his protective bubble, anyone who wants to talk to her must go through him first."

Poggibonsi thinks about that for a few minutes.

"I'll tell you what's bothering me, Shawn. The fact that Salazar placed this reporter on administrative leave from the grand jury, and put her in his office, under the pretext of an investigation. You know what they say, if the briber wants to get in touch, he might be brave enough to come waltzing into the building again. Why wouldn't the briber approach her if she is in Salazar's office. No reception center on that floor. To me, this is all a pretext. Pure bullshit.

"This is what I think. He's got a thing for this woman, obvious from the beginning when they started working together seven years ago. She had met up with him several times, leaving her car at the parking garage so she could drive with him. Does Salazar think we're not watching?"

"They did go back to the office together plenty of times," Schneider says. "I had to go up there to pick up a package; the two of them were going through a stack of files after that Midas murder.

"Shawn, Shawn, my boy, pretext, it's all pretext for them getting in bed with one another. Isn't your nose working these days? I mean, you're getting soft, buddy. My nose tells me these two were in a huddle way before the game even got started. You'll see! Mark my words."

"She's married to the other guy, the one who worked here years ago."

"Yeah, I know all about him. Vince. He's a nice guy, but his head's up his ass. He's a workaholic. The man never stays home one day or has ever taken this woman and kids on vacation. I dated her best friend Jolie for a few months, you know, just casual. I hear the family hasn't taken a full week's vacation since he's opened the agency that hires freelance reporters. The man does nothing but work. She's too hot a chick to be left to her own devices."

"Hey, kid, maybe you just solved this case. What if it was the husband who left the attempted bribe to scare his wife back into his bed. You never know! I'm going to look at the vouchered envelope again. I think there's something with the envelope, the hundred-dollar bills, and that note, I can't put my finger on. Why don't we take a trip over to the property clerk office? I don't think we'll be wasting our time."

Before the Property Clerk's office opened officially the following morning, two under-cover detectives strolled into the office, unhooked the chain that blocked the entrance, at the bottom level of the District Attorney's office building.

A tall thin African-American woman, with short bleached yellow hair, stood behind the counter smiling. Silvia Jackson was dressed in an NYPD blue uniform, on which hung a dozen or more citations pinned to her chest.

"What brings you guys to my neck of the woods?" Silvia asked.

"Silvia, my darling!" Poggi said.

"Detective Poggi, what can I do you for?" Silvia flashed her sparkling teeth and prepared herself for the Poggi and Schneider show, whatever routine they were going to perform, they had decided to foist it upon her today.

"Shawn, would you get a look at this girl's medals. Is there anything she hasn't been decorated with since the beginning of the New York City Police Department?" Shawn picked up on Poggi's banter.

"You know, Poggi, Silvia doesn't give me the time of day unless I'm with you. What do you think that's all about? You know what I think, don't you? I think she's hot for you, my friend." All three go hysterical.

"Ah, shucks, detectives, you make me swoon all over myself," Shawn fakes Silvia's voice.

"Oh, yeah, I've got a thing for him all right, it's packed right here in my holster. She's grabs on to her police-issued Glock, placing it in a chock hold.

"I guess we better get down to business," Poggi said, "this woman is way too tough for us."

Poggi goes forward filling out the required requisite, using the pen attached to a chain at the counter. He slides it across to Silvia, requesting the original envelope that had been vouchered after it had become property of the NYPD from the hands of Jay Larkin at Chase Bank dated June 23, 1999. The envelope that had once contained a vast amount of hundred-dollar-bills, the alleged attempted bribe of one Grand Jury reporter, Lana Lewis.

"Now that I think about it, it might be filed under Marie-Elaina Lewis, her proper name," Poggi said.

"You're the second one this week who has asked to see that piece of evidence," Silva said. The two detectives looked at one another, as Silvia made her way to the back of the pigeonholes, opening a desk drawer, pulling out the requisite that Salazar had filled out the morning before.

"Salazar," Poggi said to Shawn Schneider, in a whisper. "He signed it out yesterday morning, probably while we were talking with Niccolo Junior. I wonder what that's all about."

Silva, who was now wearing rubber gloves, came out from behind a stack of file drawers with a box containing the envelope, the vouchered hundred-dollar bills in a in a see-through hard plastic. The writing on the front said the envelope indicated that the envelope had contained $15,000. The bribe note was put in a separate plastic showing the details of the worded letter. The original white envelope with Marie-Elaina Lewis's name was also saved in see-through plastic tucked inside an evidence box --the had been segregated into the zip-locked bags.

Silvia asked, "Detectives, do you want me to set you up in one of the rooms so you can view the evidence in private?"

Jack glanced over at his partner. Shawn shrugged his shoulders, not understanding Poggi's body language.

He whispered, "I'd love to see how the bills fit inside the original envelope. I'm trying to decide, Shawn, whether $15,000 could have fit comfortably in there. Or was it a tight fit. Or was there room for another ten grand?"

"If I remember correctly," his partner said, "Ms. Lewis's original statement indicated she'd guess $5,000 in bills. Afterwards she had thought about the thickness of the envelope, and changed her count to $7,000 or $8,000, could have been contained in that envelope. She didn't know because she had never counted the money."

"I can't do that for you, Detectives," Silvia said, overhearing their conversation. "I'm not permitted to touch the bills."

"No problem, Silvia."

Poggi, determined to add more wood on the fire of seeking out evidence in what he hopes to be a case against a court reporter, turns to Schneider, and says, "I have another idea, Shawn. Let's go pay Jay Larkin a visit at Chase Bank."

The younger detective shakes his head, fully cognizant, that could be a big no-no, making an unauthorized visit to a potential suspect; he urges Poggi back to the Salazar's office to report the outcome of their visit to Junior Giovanni.

Dropped

One word,

then another,

they fall like shooting stars,

out of the atmosphere,

gone from my fingers,

from my mind,

lost forever!

PART IV

COSTA AND
AGNES REUNITE

CHAPTER 1

After Detectives Poggibonsi and Schneider split from the bakery, leaving Junior now concerned with his mother, still sitting outside in the hot sun, Junior strutted outside to check on her.

"Mama, enough Vitamin D today?" he asked.

"*Scusi?*" Agnes asked, lapsing into Italian, fuzzy from having fallen asleep.

"Sun, Mama. Too much sun?"

"No, I'm okay," she answered. After Junior goes back into the bakery, Agnes calls out for him.

"*Una favore*, son, maybe I should sit in the shade. I'mma too hot. Sorry, *figlio mio*, you are correct."

Junior smiled inwardly. *Some days she understands English, and some days she doesn't have any idea what I'm talking about, whether it's in Italian or English.*

Dutifully Junior reaches for the long iron pole alongside the edge of the awning. He catches the hook inside the mechanism, turning the awning with his muscular arms as its screeches digs into his brain.

He helps his mother from the chair and walks her into the shade. She waits to be seated again in the shade. As another annoying sound from scrapping the chair along the concrete sidewalk causes Junior to roll his eyes.

After he seats Agnes, he notices her stained housedress, that she hadn't changed her clothes from going to the park and feeding the pigeons. He thinks back to a time when she wouldn't be caught dead outside of the house if she wasn't fashionably dressed. His stepfather had spent hundreds of dollars buying her the best clothing in high-end stores. If he wasn't sick, he'd see that she looked like a bag lady. Big Nick enjoyed his years with Agnes raising him, fussing over her, he saw that as a privilege, not has something he had to do because he had married her when she needed someone to love her and care for her. That had all ended when Costa came back to find her in the Brooklyn bakery.

It wasn't him returning to the scene of the crime, to his bastard son, where he and Maria, a month after they were married had come and opened the first of the Brooklyn bakeries. He said he had come to make his apologies. It was from that day to today, almost fifteen years now, Junior noticed his mother's downfall. At first, it was sleeping later in the mornings. Then she started to forget to take her medication – an antidepressant – she had to religiously take, according to her doctor.

Big Nick had never held a grudge against Costa for not manning up during Agnes's pregnancy. He realized Costa was a scared boy. Manning up would have meant losing Maria and

Mario's generous offer of a percent of the bakery. Costa had only done what hundreds of other boys had over the years. He panicked.

Costa's past lies discouraged Agnes' will to live. And after he had moved away from Brooklyn, putting effort into his life with Maria and their young daughter, to try staring his life with Maria and their daughter. He had given up everything he had worked for, not to be found out by his father-in-law, Mario.

After covering his tracks, ten years had gone by, Lana had begun to understand her father's devious ways and Costa made her life as miserable as he had made her mother's.

"You're a liar," he'd bark. "Always covering for your mother. One day, you'll see, lying is going to strike you down. Don't come looking for me to get you out of trouble."

*****

If it wasn't for a newspaper article, Agnes might have never known about the two females who had earned jobs as court stenographers, who were now working alongside homicide detectives, in one of the city's first initiatives to hire women with equal-pay opportunities.

The reporter who had written the piece, James Grant, praised Lana Lewis and Joline Wilson, for being able to stare down homicide scenes right in the face with the same professionalism as their counterparts. He called their body language "I see a kind of grit in these women, like John Wayne, tackling a situation," -- witnessing and being part of gruesome homicide scenes, aiding detectives and prosecutors, taking statements and testimony in some of the most horrific places, making it into news headlines and on network news stations.

After having knowledge of his mother's reading of the column, Junior knew his mother, with the knowledge that Lana Lewis was less than a mile from the bakery, he had seen with his own eyes, Agnes becoming deranged in her thinking.

She constantly looked like she was plotting, talking to herself. She had stopped wearing nice clothing; she no longer cared about how she looked walking on Court Street. She had stopped going to the beauty parlor. She looked like a woman possessed with more important things on her mind.

Junior's fear was that his mother might contemplate carrying out an act of revenge against Lana, his step-sister. The fear of her going forward after so many years with the vendetta she had had against her own cousin Maria Sparta. She wanted to get even with the woman who had caused her a life of misery. Agnes's desire for revenge had become more palpable after Costa had given her $20,000 to bring to his daughter, Lana, beg her, from her father, for forgiveness. The "so-called-bribe", the envelope brimming with hundreds of dollar bills.

Junior had overheard the conversation that his mother and Costa had discussed early one morning, when they thought he was asleep in his room.

Costa begged her, "Agnes, I need for you to speak with my daughter on my behalf," probably as he shoved the envelope in her hand. "I want to pay back my daughter for the years I had been absent in her life; give her this money. It's what Arturo had given to me for her on the day of her baptism."

Then Junior heard Costa pacing back and forth in the kitchen, hoping he'd be able to convince Agnes. As walked from the kitchen into the foyer, hoping to convince her, "You say this: I don't expect forgiveness. I don't expect anything in return. Please, Agnes," he saw Costa down on his knees when he opened the door of his bedroom. "I need you to do this for me."

Even though Agnes had married Big Nick when Junior was a baby, Junior had known she had adored him. When Costa returned, the hurt somehow surfaced, and Agnes wanted her revenge.

Against Nick's wishes, Agnes had decided to carry out this task that she had twisting in her stomach a long time ago. She tasted the bitterness in her mouth like the spoiled wine that had been put on a sponge and placed on Jesus' tongue as he hung on the cross.

Junior despised his part in all of this. The knowledge of his mother's act made him an accomplice, as guilty as he had been all along in his father's illegal numbers organization.

Junior needed to make a good confession. He had preached this idea to his mother and tried to

steer her away from carrying out her plan to bribe Lana. He had known it was wrong and yet he continued to take a role in his mother's obvious insanity. Because of having been raised in a convent and being around nuns as a small child, he had frequented the sacraments of the church. At this time in his life, he wanted to free his soul from the burden baring down on him like a bolder pressing against his chest.

Confessing his sins to Father Sal in the secrecy and sanctity of confession, Junior believed his mother's acts would not be revealed. That was something a priest wasn't permitted to divulge.

While he felt less than uplifted that a murder had not been committed, he still wasn't aware of what his mother's ultimate intentions were. He wanted no part of being her co-conspirator. He couldn't bring himself to tell Nick, the man he hated to disappoint, a man he would always adore.

PART V

GOOD ADVICE

CHAPTER 1

ather Salvatore LoBianco entered the seminary on his eighteenth birthday, some fifteen years ago. When he first became a parish priest at Saint Mary's, Father Sal, as he was referred to, set up a youth group, confraternity, like the old days of the 1950s. Teenagers exchanged music, dance steps, and sometimes broke the rules and snuck in a bottle of beer.

When Junior joined the group, he was happy to have friends his own age, and another strong male figure in Father Sal.

Sal wore his Franciscan robes and carried his crucifix on his neck like sporting a thick gold chain. He had made is mother proud, not his father so much, who considered his son a talented musician and had hoped Sal would follow in his footsteps as a classical guitarist. After a one-year stint in Julliard, Sal boxed his guitar and went away into the seminary. Since the guitar, his most-bestowed gift from his parents, was visiting Saint Francis of Assisi, his patron saint; the patron said of all Friars. Sal wore his balding crown like a halo, he loved the priesthood and enjoyed the camaraderie of the teenagers.

They trusted him. In today's day and age, that said a lot for teenagers.

Outside on the back patio, sitting at a picnic table under a flowering tree, Father Sal and Junior were discussing Agnes. They were interrupted momentarily when the housekeeper came out to tell Father Sal he had a phone call. Claire handed Junior a glass of lemonade and left one for the priest. Junior sipped at the tart yellow liquid and expressed a sour face, put the glass down on the wooden table he sat at.

Father Sal came back looking forlorn.

"What?" asked Junior.

"Your mother is going to call an ambulance for your father. He's having difficulty breathing."

Junior bunked his legs trying to get them out from under the table. He bolted through the garden area and out through the wrought iron gate. Father Sal followed him.

Two blocks over from Saint Mary's, on the corner of Van Brunt and the highway, four or five people had gathered. They were workers from the bakery and people who had lived in the neighborhood a long time. Everyone knew everyone else.

Junior and the priest found Agnes sitting in a chair holding her husband's hand alongside Big Nick's bed, who didn't look as bad as Junior thought he might have.

"He started gagging on his saliva," Agnes reported. "I got scared."

"It's okay," Father Sal assured her. "Let the attendants come up and look at him." Junior hadn't said anything yet to his mother. Agnes was prone to exaggeration, jumping to conclusions, always thinking Big Nick was going to die at any second. The eighty-year old man had been on chemo treatment for the past six weeks and things were bound to turn up. But today was a false alarm in Junior's mind.

After the emergency doctor from Methodist Hospital checked Nick Giovanni's breathing, his heart, his lung function, he felt there was no reason to move Nick to the hospital.

Agnes felt mortified. Father Sal patted her hand and blessed Nick's forehead with a drop of oil from a small bottle he had removed from his pocket. Junior felt relieved. After a brief stay by Nick's bedside, the man looked bewildered as to the commotion, he gave the priest a half smile, and shooed him away with his right hand.

"You go, Father. Thank you." He lifted his head slightly from the pillow and plopped back it down and closed his eyes. Junior, who hadn't said a word, pissed at his mother for causing him to get excited over nothing, left Agnes and Nick, as they had found them, her holding his hand at his bedside.

Father Sal and Junior continued their conversation outside the bakeshop, taking their place out of the sun's direct rays, at an ice cream parlor table.

"Her guilt is catching up with her," Junior said to the priest. "She made one mistake after the other and now she believes my father is going to pay for her sins. I know how she thinks.

"Let me put your heart at rest, Niccolo," the priest said. Calling Junior Niccolo sounded formal and Junior waited for the other shoe to drop.

"What was your part in this bribe? What did you do with your own hands? Or voice? Did you threaten this woman, I guess we could say, your stepsister?"

"Not exactly."

"Be clear, Niccolo, I'll have no part in helping you if you don't tell me the truth."

"My mother thinks I disguised my voice and called the court reporter. You know, used a scare tactic. But I didn't. The only thing I did do was scope out the building when I had to appear in the grand jury in the Supreme Court building. I asked someone where the prosecutor's office was. I walked through the park to the DA's building, and told my mother about the exits, the steps leading up and down to the third floor, the court reporters' offices, instead of taking the elevator. There were a few people in the cubicles and I merely said I was lost."

"Did you place the envelope that contained the bribe-money in the court reporter's mailbox?"

"No, definitely not. My mother thinks I scared her with my voice – pretending I was a tough guy. Nothing more. Well, just the steps – which office was Lana's. I knew it was her, after the newspaper article – you know, it was all spelled out in the Daily News, 'homicide division trains women,' something along those lines."

"You're going to have to man up. When you came to the rectory today, before your mother called, you were saying something about two detectives."

"Yeah, well, those two guys were fishing around. I mean, that's their job. They asked me if I knew a court reporter. I said, no, I didn't."

"You lied to them?"

"Is that really lying? I don't know her." Father Sal stood up – he looked disgusted by Junior's answer. "She's your stepsister, how can you say you don't know her?"

"I don't know her. I've never seen her in my life. I mean, except the newspaper article." Sal took pause to leave Junior sitting at the table looking like a goofy teenager who had gotten caught smoking pot, choking on his words, as smoke curled out of his nose.

CHAPTER 2

W orking side by side, Lana and Salazar had had many conversations. They talked about everyday things, subjects unrelated to people or gangsters of Organized Crime. One Monday Salazar tried to throw Lana off guard by asking her this question.

"Do you know the name Costa Lewis?"

Hearing her father's name coming out of Salazar's mouth, Lana believed she'd never have the satisfaction of knowing whether she could ever convince Salazar that she had no direct knowledge of this man. The man they called "A Louie," a known racketeer and an enforcer for the Giovannis.

"If you're asking me that question, you already know he's my father. What kind of trouble is he in now?" Lana didn't give Peter a chance to answer.

"I haven't seen him since I was ten years old. We are only related by blood and nothing else. He's a sonofabitch. That's what I know."

Salazar knew mostly everything about her. And he had tried to keep his mouth shut because Lana wasn't responsible for her father's sins. But those sins had followed her whether she liked it or not. He shoved the paper in his hand back into the file folder and picked up his cup, sipping coffee and looking in her eyes.

Lana knew one thing about Salazar, which she had heard many times from co-workers. If this was a time for honestly, she'd like to know why he had never been married. She also knew his decision on not getting married was much to his mother's dissatisfaction. He had told her on occasion that his mother wanted grandchildren, like most mothers do. Peter had shared that with her having a late dinner at their respective desks. He had said he didn't have the temperament to marry and raise children. He had grown up in his parents' home with three younger brothers and had had enough babysitting experience to last him a lifetime.

"Let my brothers do the honors in making my mother a grandmother," Salazar had said one evening while they spoke casually.

Lana had often believed she had seen the real Peter Salazar that night as a handsome self-centered player. Maybe he was gay and had decided to remain in the closet. Sitting next to him, she realized she had never seen him with a woman, nor had she ever noticed any entries in his diary, like dinner dates or cocktails with a woman's name attached.

She thought about the first day they had met when Rob had taken her up to his office to introduce her to the young detective. The one who would become her mentor. She was taken by him that day, although she never thought of him as Detective Peter Salazar, an extremely good-looking man who dressed to the nines, while others in the DA's office wore blue jeans.

He had made an impact on the D.A.'s office and rose up in the ranks to bureau chiefs before she was working there five years. Not until she wondered into his office feeling sick and disgusted with herself for not having trusted him, going to him with her problems after receiving the so-called bribe.

Over the years, Peter had been open with Lana, sharing memories of his parents, coming from Mexico City in the early nineteen-sixties. He had enjoyed Lana being interested in his life. He explained his parents had come to America around the time he had started grammar school, which confirmed one of Lana's earlier hunches about him; he had loved his father and that she couldn't relate to.

Salazar had spoken of how hard his father had worked when they first came, breaking his back as a laborer in the more affluent neighborhoods of Flatbush, where they had hired Salazar's father to do gardening and landscaping.

Years later, the father had started his own business and had warned his oldest son, Peter, that if he didn't make his way in America by going to school and getting good grades, his father had promised them he'd go back to Mexico with the money he had earned, and they could be peasants again. It probably wasn't a true story, but Peter had goals. His father put it in his head, "You *will* become a lawyer, my son."

"Well, at least your father saw your potential," Lana snapped, "as a capable person who was smart enough to go to college. My father thought I was an idiot." Salazar looked at Lana, an odd expression appeared on his face. He didn't like her being disrespectful, verbalizing her hatred, as she had on several other occasions discussing her father. It had turned Salazar off.

"I'm sorry," she said, "I didn't get along with my father. He busted my buns from the time I learned how to walk, until I finally stopped paying attention to him."

"And how did that go for you?" Salazar asked her in a snarky tone. Lana laughed. Salazar's interest in her life-story felt impossible to answer. She wondered why he cared. Yet, she'd have to admit, it felt good that he cared about her, even if it was negative. She hadn't had anyone interested in her life since – well, since high school, since Vince came along. And Rob too, the man who had spent a lot of time training her to be an excellent court reporter.

Lana watched Salazar's mannerisms, all proud of himself, drinking a cup of coffee while she juggled his color-coded files: reminding herself, the red ones were for murder suspects; blue for the gang-bangers and organized drug offenders, the real kingpins of the streets in Brooklyn; purple for organized crime, loan-sharking, the dockworkers who beat up other dockworkers to whom they had loaned money if the "vig" wasn't paid every week.

"You are a good son, Peter," she said. "My father only wanted me as his stool pigeon. He wanted me to rat out my mother who hadn't done anything wrong to him her whole life. She did her job, kept our home the way he demanded, did the laundry, cooking, cleaning, and then going out midafternoons scrubbing dirty hallway floors to make an extra five dollars a day.

"My father had a fixation that my mother disappeared when I was in school, had gone on bus trips and he questioned me occasionally if I went along with her. Always asking me, did I know where she had gone. He wanted something from me I couldn't give him, knowledge of my mother's actions. Not whether I had knowledge for college, but only the good sense to spy on my mother."

"Did your mother take those bus trips?" Lana couldn't believe Salazar asked her that question. *Were all men nuts?*

"No, "she said. "He had this guilt – whatever you want to call it. He left us before I was ten years old. By that time, I didn't care. We sold our furniture, moved back to Brooklyn and lived with my grandmother, and my mother continued to work two jobs to contribute something towards the rent and help put food on the table.

"I know where you're coming from, idolizing your father. When I think about who my daughters idolize, I'd have to say it's me because I've always been there for them. Not their father. Sure, they're spoiled. They also attended private school, because Vince and I did nothing but work, work, work and more work. Listen, I'm not complaining," she said, "It's just not fair."

"What's not fair, Lana? That you had a sonofabitch for a father? Life's not fair sometimes. I'm sure you know that. Look at your situation." She prepared herself for battle on what might next come out of his mouth. This bright young man with a lawyer's disposition, he had thought he could rattle her. Older men like her father had tried, and she'd not let anyone do that to her again.

If she had to wager she'd bet Salazar was about six years or seven years younger than she was. That would make him too young in her books for any real common sense. Lana wondered where he thought he came off knowing anything about anything, especially about her.

"What about my situation, Peter? It's been four months, going on five months now? Do you want to ask me that question again? You don't have to ask because I'm going to tell you. I had never any thought of keeping the money, accepting the so-called bribe we've talked about until we've turned blue in the face. None. I'm clear about that in my own head now."

"Now? That means you had to think about it before it became clear to you?" he asked. She gave him a disgusted look, her tiny nose flared, her face flushed. She threw the files on the desk, got up and tried to leave the room.

Salazar grabbed her arm. "Listen, Lana, I'm not accusing you of anything. You act like such a tough guy. You think you're so street smart. A cool cucumber. Okay, girl, so you came from Brooklyn. Well, lady, so did I. Are you fucking kidding me, you bring a stack of hundred-dollar bills to your husband's friend, the vice president of a bank, no less. I know you're not a stupid woman. But you didn't even know how much money was in the envelope and you had handed the whole thing over. What were you thinking?"

His words, some of which rang true, struck Lana to her core. She felt the floodgates open. She might look tough and could carry her weight with any man. But her downfall was always her sensitive side, the emotions always found their way out through her eyes. And her emotions were now close to the surface.

Maybe crying, sobbing, yelling, might have worked with her mother – and it hadn't even worked with her – it certainly wasn't going to work with Salazar.

"What do you want from me?" Lana untangled herself from his hold. "You'd go great with my husband. You should talk with him because he doubts me, too. What about Detective Poggi, didn't he interrogate Junior Giovanni? You guys don't get it. I was the fucking messenger!"

CHAPTER 3

L ana had had enough. She took to the street, forgetting to call Vince, who would be picking her up after work.

She started her trek in deep thought, walking south on Court Street; as she passed women's clothing stores, she looked in the windows. Where there were racks outside on sale items, she touched garments, looked at price tags and then resumed her walk.

By the time she had gotten to the overpass for the Brooklyn-Queens Expressway, she had journeyed about a mile into a neighborhood that had looked familiar, somewhere she might have been as a child.

Lana stopped short of crossing in front of a moving car on Columbia Street. She apologized to the driver of the blue vehicle by mouthing the word "sorry". Her slim body, protected under her red woolen cape, gave her an air of elegance.

"It's okay," the older man said from his open car window. "Wish I was daydreaming with you." Lana smiled and probably made the old guy's day. She was her prettiest when she was her saddest. Something about her pale eyes and ginger hair that captivated strangers to stop and look at her. She found it odd and never thought of herself as an attractive woman. All stemming from a poor-self-image as a teenager, and most likely continued to occur into her adulthood.

When Lana became pregnant after she and Vince had been intimate, she had blown up like a balloon, her face growing out of proportion; her body much heavier than her five-foot frame could tolerate. Not realizing she was carrying twins, Lana gave up trying to be attractive. She let her hair get straggly and stopped wearing makeup. She had even started court reporting college looking like a stuffed oven-roasted chicken.

It wasn't until Peter Salazar, who constantly made a fuss over her, that she began to believe in herself again. After their little tiff that afternoon, questions circulated in and out of Lana's head while walking.

ABOUT THE AUTHOR

Patricia A. Florio has dedicated her life to storytelling, advocacy, and giving a voice to the voiceless. With a background in journalism and a deep commitment to her community, Patricia's work reflects her passion for meaningful connections and her unwavering belief in the power of words. Through her stories, she aims to inspire, uplift, and empower others. Her own journey has been one of resilience, compassion, and unwavering dedication to her craft. *The Word Catcher* marks the beginning of Patricia's published journey, bringing her insights and reflections to readers worldwide.